A LOVE SO GOOD 3

The Chamber Brothers

K. RENEE

KASH

Eva and I were on our way to the party when I got the call from Lonnie saying that Cas' mom called the restaurant saying that Nas and Cas were in trouble. Pulling up on Nas' street, there were police cars everywhere.

"Oh, my God! What is going on?" Eva questioned as we jumped out of the car. I ran up to his gate, but the cop stopped me before I could get to my son's car.

"Sir, I'm going to have to ask you to step back," he said to me.

"This is my son's house!" I told his ass. I needed to know what the hell was going on with my damn son.

"Come right this way, sir," he stated, and I followed him to the ambulance. I could hear Nas cursing, and I let out a sigh of relief. If he was going off the way he was I knew his injuries were minor.

"Nas!" I called out as I approached the back of the ambulance.

"Man, be your ass careful! That shit hurt like a muthafucka!" Nas yelled at the paramedic.

"Mr. Chamber, you said you have no idea who would want to do this to you?" The cop asked Nas.

"Nope, I don't know shit, but I know this-" I cut his ass off because I knew what was coming out of his mouth next. He had a lot of blood coming from his arm.

"How bad is it?" I asked the medic.

"He was hit in the arm twice, once in his shoulder, and a bullet grazed the side of his head. When we found him, he was not conscious. I'm positive that came from him hitting his head or his body going through shock. Sir, he really needs to go to the hospital, but he refuses to leave," the paramedic stated.

"Nigga, I told yo' ass I'm fine. You're sitting here telling my pop the shit ain't gone change a muthafuckin' thing, with yo' snitch ass. Pop, he said the bullets went straight through. This shit hurt like a muthafucka, but a nigga good on the hospital shit. His ass just needs to clean me up, give me some Neosporin, and some damn Percocets. I should be good with that; I got shit to do." I shook my head at this boy. Looking around because I didn't see Cas, I just noticed her mother standing off to the side in tears.

"Where is Cas?" I questioned, and her mom looked at Nasir.

"She had a run to make," Nas spoke up. But that shit sounded off to me. He winced out in pain again, and I knew he needed to get this shit looked at.

"Nas, you need to get this checked out. You don't want this shit to get worse. If your arm gets infected, then you will have more issues. I will follow you down to the hospital," I said to him, just as my phone ring started ringing. It was my mom, and I ignored the call. I would call her back in a few minutes.

"Nah, fuck that! Pop, on some real shit, fuck this arm. I don't give a fuck if that bitch was hanging on by a thread! He gone have to clean it and wrap me up right here. I got some shit I need to handle. So, get to cleaning and wrapping, nigga!" He yelled at the paramedic. It just hit me that Priest wasn't here.

"Where the fuck is your brother? I called him and told him to come check on you?" I asked him.

"I haven't seen him," Nas stated, as he winced in pain again.

"Mr. Chamber, we will be doing a full investigation. If you can remember anything, give us a call," the cop spoke, handing him a card and walking off. My mom was calling me again, and I decided to answer because I knew her ass wasn't gone stop.

"Mom, I'm in the middle of something. Can I call you right back?" I asked her.

"Kashas, someone is in the house," she whispered.

"Say what?" I questioned.

"I need you to come right now. I was going downstairs to get another slice of cake, and I heard yelling. Priest needs help, they have guns, and you need to get your ass here now," she whispered, but I heard exactly what she said. I walked away from all the cops, so I could say what I needed to say without them hearing me.

"Mom, I need you to take Sasha and go into Priest's saferoom. You know where it is, I need you to go in there now! Do you remember the code?" I asked her.

"Yes, I know what it is," she said.

"There are guns in there, if for whatever reason you need to protect yourself, you open fire on they ass. I'm on my way now," I said, ending the call, just as the medic finished working on Nas.

"Fuckkkkkkk! Somebody is in your brother's house with guns. Eva will stay here with you and Cas' mom. I have to go handle this shit; these niggas want to fuck with my family, now I'm gone fuck with them!" I roared. I can't believe all of this bullshit was happening.

"Nigga, I know damn well you don't think I'm gone sit here while my brother is in trouble, and a nigga done snatched my fuckin' girl! Whoever fuckin' shot at me got Cas, and I'm not doing shit until my girl is safe. It's killing season around this bitch. I'm not playing no games 'bout mine. Nobody in this city is fuckin' safe, and that's my muthafuckin' word!

"What the fuck do you mean, somebody has Cas?" I asked him, and her mother burst into tears. Eva walked over and wrapped her arms around her.

"Cas' mom said when they heard the shots, Cassie ran out screaming my name. I thought I heard her screaming, but I wasn't sure because of all the gunshots. I was shooting back until I got hit, but I don't remember too much more after that. Ma Crystal said she was watching from the window and saw them snatch Cas and throw her into a truck. She said she ran out of the house, but it was too dark to get the tag on the truck.

"Let's go." I walked off, dialing up Cannon.

"Yeah," he said answering the call.

"I need you to meet me at Priest crib; we got trouble," was all I said to him and then I hung up. I was able to make it to Priest's house in under ten minutes. Pulling up by the gates, Nas and I got out of the car, and I told Eva to take Cas' mom back to my house and wait. Once they pulled off, Nas and I pulled our guns out and walked up to the house.

"Isn't that Zoey getting out of the car?" Nas asked.

"Yeah. Shit! We can't let her go into the house." I took off running to stop Zoey from going up the steps.

"Zoey," I called out in a low tone. She turned, and when she noticed that it was us, a smile spread across her face.

"Hey, Pop, Nas. I thought you guys would be at the party by now." Her expression immediately changed when she noticed Nas.

"Zoe, I need you to get back in your car and go to my

house. I need you to leave now and we will be there shortly," I told her, pulling her away from the steps.

"Why would I do that? Priest is waiting for me. Is everything alright?" She nervously questioned.

"Zoe, baby girl, you gone have to get away from here now. Some niggas is in this house with guns on my brother, and if something happens to you in the process, he would go off. Go to Pop's house, and I promise you we will get him, Big Mama, and Sasha out of here." I was trying to hold that information from her, but I guess Nas was ready for her to go.

"Oh my God, I can't leave them." She began to cry, and we pulled her to her car because time was not on our side.

"Zoey, I just sent you my address, I need you to go there right now. Eva and Crystal are there waiting on you. I promise you we will get them out of this, but I need for you to get out of here," I said to her. I'm glad she got into the car and backed out of the driveway without argument.

"Pop, I have the keys. I think we should go in through the back. Cannon just called and said he will be here in a few minutes, but we can't wait on him," Nas spoke, and we headed to the back of the house. There was no damn way that I was waiting on no damn body to go in and help my family.

Chapter Two

PRIEST

I was so fuckin' pissed I could spit fire on these niggas right now! I can't believe these niggas and this heartless ass bitch was standing in my shit, holding these fuckin' guns in my face.

"I hope you know that none of you niggas will make it out of this alive!" I yelled.

"Nigga, fuck you. We gone kill you, take your money, and my girl taking her daughter back, pussy ass nigga!" He roared, slamming his gun down the side of my face. The pain took me down for a second, and I stood back up because I would never let these pussy ass niggas see me sweat.

"You gone have to kill me, nigga! There is no way in hell that I would let you get next to my daughter. And bitch, you better make sure I'm dead because I'm definitely gone kill your ass. You had me raise a baby that wasn't even my damn child. You one fucked up, heartless ass bitch!" I looked at Keisha because I swear, I'm ripping that bitch's heart right out of her fucking chest.

"Damn, she wasn't your baby? To be honest, I didn't know whose baby she was, nor did I give a fuck. I guess it don't matter because Maz is dead." This nothing ass bitch shrugged like everything was all good.

"Bitch!" I charged at her, and Dom put his gun to my head. His bitch ass brother looked nervous, holding his damn gun. I didn't give a fuck what happened to me as long as Sasha, and Big Mama were safe. I knew that Zoey would be pulling up soon, and I had to figure this shit out before she got here.

"You're the stupid nigga for trusting a bitch like me. I may not have succeeded before in killing you and that lil' bitch you call your daughter, but I'm gone make sure both of you die today. How does it feel to know that you can't do anything to save her? I know she's in this house somewhere... Fuck-kkkkkk! We didn't check the house," Keisha said, looking at Dom.

"Fuck! Get something so we can tie his ass up. Marlo, go look in the kitchen for something," he told Marlo, but just as Marlo walked out, he was walking back in, dropping his gun to the floor. My eyes grew big as hell because Big Mama had two AK's, one in each hand. One pointed on Marlo and the other pointed at us. I was a little fuckin' nervous 'cause my damn Grandma can't shoot.

"Back the fuck away from my damn grandson, or it's gone

be some muthafuckin' problems and misunderstandings in this bitch. Lord have mercy. Keisha, you so damn stupid. You got the nerve to bring your ass in here, messing with this boy, and he ain't thinking about your ass. Now you about to get your slow ass a one-way ticket to hell. And who these dumb, slow niggas you got following your ass up? Boy, didn't I tell you to step away from my goddamn grandson!" Big Mama yelled, and she didn't even look uneasy holding the guns.

"Bitch, you need to take your old ass back where you came f..." Big Mama didn't say shit. She just started busting the damn gun all around the damn room. We all hit the fuckin' floor, quick as hell. Her ass didn't give a damn that I was in the line of fire; she just opened up on all our asses.

"Big Mama, what the hell are you doing?" I heard Nas' voice, and I let out a sigh of relief when I saw him and Pop in the room.

"This punk-ass lil' boy called me a bitch and had a gun on my grandson. Y'all asses were taking too damn long to come help my damn grandson. I had to take matters into my own hands. He could've been dead by the time y'all got here. Priest, get up, baby, and let Big Mama look at you," she said. I stood up and grabbed the gun from Dom, kicking that nigga in his fuckin' head over and over again.

"Yo' Rambo wannabe, non-shooting ass almost killed your damn grandson," Nas told her.

"Bitch, you thought it was safe to come fuck with me in my fuckin' home! Putting my fuckin' family in danger!" I roared and beat the shit out of this nigga. I didn't stop beating his ass until my Pop called my name.

"Priest, who will my daughter have if you kill me? She's not your fucking daughter!" Keisha yelled, and I gripped her ass up with my gun to her head, ready to pull the trigger.

"Bitch, shut the fuck up! You were never a mother to her. Your evil ass tried to kill your own fucking daughter for money! Help me understand how the fuck does she need you? She's better off with a perfect stranger than to be in the presence of a conniving, money-hungry, stupid ass bitch, like you. No matter what the fuck the test results say, THAT'S MY MUTHAFUCKIN' DAUGHTER! If anybody tries to take her or bring harm to her, they ass is gone die! Fuck you and your fucking miserable ass life, bitch!" I roared. I was so fucking pissed It felt like fire was rolling off my damn tongue.

"Priest, not here, son. Your grandmother and daughter are in the house," Pop spoke, and that calmed me a little. I swear it took everything in me not to blow this bitch's brain all over these fucking walls. Cannon and some of our men walked into the room with their guns up and ready.

"Take these pussy ass bitches out of here and take them to the warehouse," Nas told them.

"Ma, where is Sasha?" I asked her.

"I put her in the safe room," she said. Pop and I took off upstairs to check on my daughter. When I made it to the safe room, Sasha was inside playing with her toys. I'm so happy that my baby girl was good. A few minutes later, Nas came walking into the room. I noticed the bandages and blood on my brother's arm, and it just hit me that I was supposed to be going to check on him.

"Nas, what the fuck happened?" I asked him.

"I had a run-in with Cas' ex at the club a few nights ago, and I think he followed one of us home. It's the ex that had her setting niggas up; you know the story about that. I was leaving home, and my car got shot up, Cas heard the shots and got snatched up. That's why I believe that it was his ass. I got Cannon working on locating this nigga for me, and Cam and his crew are on their way down," he explained.

"Nas, why aren't you getting this shit checked out? How many times did you get hit?" I asked because his ass was bleeding through the bandages.

"Twice, but I'm not getting shit looked at until me and my fuckin' girl getting this shit checked out together. Fuck that. The longer I wait, the more danger she's in, and if something happens to Cas, I swear I'm finding every living muthafucka in that nigga's family and killing they ass. My girl is my fuckin' life, and I'm not gone be right until she's right!" Nas snapped, and I could understand how he feels.

"Let's get the fuck out of here and find her. I know Zoey is gonna go crazy over this shit... Wait, where the fuck is Zoey? She should have been here by now," I asked, pulling my phone out.

"Son, calm down, I sent her to my house. Trust me, she's safe. I just checked in on them, and Eva said she was trying to get her to get some rest. I need to get Big Mama, and Sasha over there until we handle all of this bullshit we have going on." There was no way that I could be on the streets and be worried about my family. I can't express the feelings that I was going through right now. I haven't had time to process the fact that this beautiful baby girl wasn't my daughter by blood. I'm gone rip this bitch apart for what she did to me and my daughter.

"We can put them on ice while we go look for Cas," I said to Nas.

"Nahh, you need to kill them muthafuckas right fuckin' now. We not giving these bitches a chance to breathe another muthafuckin' day," Nas said as we made our way out of the room. Big Mama was waiting at the door and I told her to pack a bag for her and Sash. Our crew had already removed those pussy ass niggas out of my house.

"Nas, we got movement at one of his sister's crib," Cannon said to him.

"Pop, can you get Big Mama, and Sasha over to your house and we will meet you at the warehouse?" I requested.

"Nah, get them straight and check on Zoe. She's pregnant and we don't need shit happening to the baby. We will meet y'all at the warehouse, and don't kill that bitch Keisha until I'm there to see that shit go down. Cannon and I got this shit right here," Nas said to me.

"I got him, just make sure your daughter and grandmother are good," Cannon spoke, and he and Nas walked out. I went upstairs to change my clothes, and make sure that Big Mama and Sasha were ready to go. It took us about thirty minutes to get over to Pop's crib. Walking into the house, Zoey was talking to Cas' mom.

"Priest," she called out as she walked over to me.

"We're good, I need you to stop stressing and relax," I told her.

"Is Nas alright? Somebody kidnapped my damn cousin and we need to get her back," she cried, and I pulled her into my arms.

"I know, baby girl. We're gone get her back, I put that on my life. None of us will let anything happen to Cas. I just need you to stay calm. None of you are to leave this house. We have some guys watching the house, so you are all safe," I explained.

"Priest, we need to leave," Pop said. I kissed Zoey and we left out. I was ready to kill these niggas and get Cas back. I don't know why these fuck niggas thought it was safe to come into my shit and fuck with me. I wanted to kill they ass right then and there, but Pop was right. I couldn't do no shit like that with Sasha and my grandmother in the house. I don't give a fuck about Dom and Marlo being our cousins, just like they didn't give a fuck about running up in my shit.

Knowing that Priest, Sasha, and Big Mama were alright made me feel a little better, but I was going crazy not knowing if Cas was going to be alright. I needed them to get her out of this shit. My aunt Crystal was a complete mess, and so was I.

"Zoey, why don't you try and get some rest? Everything is going to be alright. I know my boys will find her. I sent up my prayers and Cassie gone be alright." I knew Big Mama was trying to calm me down, but there was no way that I could sleep when my cousin was out there going through God knows what.

"I can't sleep until I know that Cas is safe. Do they even know who took her?" I asked.

"I told Nas exactly what I saw, but it was dark outside. As soon as she ran out, I tried to call out for her, but she was already out the door. I looked out the window and saw a man grab her and throw her in the truck. There was a woman with him, but again, I couldn't see their faces. I just want my daughter back; she doesn't deserve any of this. I pray that Nasir can get her out of this mess," my aunt cried, and I sat down next to her, wrapping my arms around her. I know if I'm feeling this way, it had to hurt her ten times worse than it was hurting me.

"Aunt Crystal, we just have to keep the faith. I'm going to try and get some rest and pray that they find her. I think you need to get some rest as well, Eva has the guest bedroom ready for you," I said to her.

"Come on, Crystal. I can show you where everything is." My aunt followed her upstairs. I decided to lay on the couch and rest, hoping that they would come through the door soon. My phone was ringing, and the call was from a blocked number.

"Hello? Hello?" The caller hung up. I guess it was a wrong number, and I put my phone back down on the table. As soon as I closed my eyes, my phone started ringing again, and it came up as a blocked number again.

"Hello? Hello?" I spoke, but they didn't say anything.

"Stop calling my damn phone if you're not going to say anything." I was agitated and didn't have time for this shit. Just as I was about to hang up, the person started talking.

"I miss you. I'm pissed the fuck off about the shit that went down with yo' pussy ass baby daddy." I was shocked to hear Ty's voice.

"Ty, I get that you're angry, but please don't disrespect my child's father. I'm sorry about what happened, and I tried calling you to apologize for it. I don't think now is a good time for us to talk. I have some family issues going on. I miss you as a friend too, and I promise we will talk when I get back to New York." I enjoyed being friends with Ty. Now, if he could understand that I can't be anything more than just a friend to him, I would like to continue our friendship.

"I'm not gone even discuss yo' nigga, just hit me up when you're back in the city." He ended the call, but I don't know if I liked how the fuck he was talking to me. Big Mama came walking out of the room. It was going on two in the morning, so I know she had to be exhausted.

"Big Mama, are you alright?" I asked her.

"It's hard to get sleep when my boys are out there in the line of fire. I worry about them and just can't understand why trouble always seems to find my family. Don't get me wrong; I'm no fool to what they out there doing in the streets. Kashas' father was into the same shit, and to be honest, my son saw way too much growing up, and that's my fault. Even though Bianca tried her best to shield her boys from it, they still ended up in it. It was just something different about Priest. Zoey, I know that it's going to take time to forgive him, but baby, that's a good man. He's getting ready to go through a tough time, and I'm asking you to be there for him. I can't tell you about his business, but I know in the days to come, you will find out. He's going to need you more than anything he's ever needed in his life," she revealed and I was so confused.

"Big Mama, is Priest alright? You're scaring me," I asked nervously.

"He's going to be alright, and I don't mean to scare you. I'm just letting you know that when this mess is over, realization is going to set in, and he's going to need you." She stood and walked into the kitchen. I laid back on the couch as her words kept playing in my mind. I sent up a silent prayer and tried to get some sleep.

Chapter Four

CASSIE

I'm scared out of my mind, and my heart is screaming out for my man. All I can think about is Nas and seeing his car shot up. I don't know if anybody is looking for me, but I pray that they are. This nigga is fucking crazy. I knew that bitch Janelle was a fuckin' snake. She was with Black when he took me, and if I get out of this shit, I swear I'm going to kill this bitch. I have no idea where we are, but this nigga has me down in this nasty ass basement with no damn windows. I heard someone messing with the door, and I knew it was his bitch ass.

"Bitch, did you think I was going to let you be with that pussy ass nigga? Your nigga is dead, so you might as well get his ass out of your system." He grabbed me by the neck, jerking me off the floor and kissed me. I bit down on his lip, and he punched the shit out of me. That shit hurt like hell, but I needed this nigga to know that all of my thoughts were for Nas.

"I will never forget about him! I don't give a fuck what you do to me, but he will always be a part of me!" I screamed with tears falling from my eyes. He gripped me up, hitting me in my face. I tried to block a couple of his punches as I screamed out in pain. He slung me back to the floor and walked out. If I didn't find a way out of here soon, this nigga was going to kill me. I could feel my eye swelling by the second. The door opened again, and when I looked up, it was Janelle.

"You must love getting your ass beat. You need to do what the fuck he says, and shit will go easy for you." This bitch smiled, and I wanted to knock that shit off her face.

"Bitch, fuck you! You better pray I don't get out of here, because I'm killing your hoe ass, and that's on everything I love!" I yelled. She pulled her gun out, pressing it against my chin.

"Say that shit again. What you gone do to me?" She gritted out.

"Janelle, bring your ass up here!" Black screamed. She pulled the gun away from me and walked off. I had to find a way out of this shit. I know he said Nas was dead, but I refuse to believe that. My heart was connected to his, and I knew he was out there somewhere. I could feel it. I felt sick as hell, and I just couldn't hold it in any longer. I saw a bucket and jumped up to grab it just as the vomit came up out of me. I didn't know what the test results were, but deep down, I knew that I was pregnant. About an hour later, he was walking back in the room and threw a bag of food down in front of me.

"What the fuck is that smell?" He asked.

"I'm not feeling well, and I had to vomit."

"Eat that food. If you start acting like you miss a nigga, I may clean you up and move you into my bed once you get yo' shit together. I don't think my bitch would mind you joining us; she likes to suck on a good juicy pussy." He smiled, but I didn't even respond.

"I need to test that pussy out before I let her have you. I missed yo' fine ass. I should beat yo' ass again for giving that nigga my fuckin' pussy. If you act right, shit can go smooth, but if you on some bullshit know that I will kill you." He left, walking back upstairs. I knew for sure that I had to figure a way out of here because I be damned if I'm gone just sit here and let a nigga beat and rape me. There is no way that I can let that shit go down.

I knew my eye was closing up because I could barely see out of it, and the pain from my face was damn near unbearable. I was so tired, but I refuse to sleep in this fuckin' place.

God, please help me get out of this mess. I pray that you have your arms wrapped around Nasir. Amen.

I had to send up a prayer for both of us. I looked around the room to see if I could find anything that I could use to fuck these two bitches up when the time was right. I looked down at the bag of food. I was starving, but I couldn't bring myself to eat. I leaned my back against the wall to try and get some type of comfort. When my mind went to Nasir and the situation I'm in right now, I broke down crying. This was all so fucked up. I was supposed to be celebrating my birthday with my family. Now I'm sitting here worried about if I was going to live or die.

Chapter Five

NAS

Cannon and I just pulled up to this nigga Black sister's house. We weren't a hundred percent certain that this nigga had Cas, but I felt that shit in my gut. Who else would shoot my shit up and take her? He was the only problem I really had on the streets. I don't give a fuck, everybody gone die until I find my fuckin' girl.

"You ready?" Cannon asked.

"Yeah, let's do this." We got out of the car, walked up to the front door and I kicked that bitch in. Fuck knocking, and fuck easing in the back door on these bitches!

"What the fuck?!" This bitch came running into the living room with her gun raised.

"Bitch, if you don't put that bullshit ass toy gun down and tell me where the fuck your brother is!" I held my gun up, ready to blow this bitch head off.

"I don't know where my brother is, and if I did know, I wouldn't tell you niggas! The fuck you thought this shit was. You not gone just run-up in my shit! Now, if you don't get the fuck out of my house, I'm gone light yo' ass up!" She yelled.

"Bitch, you gone have to do that 'cause I ain't leaving this bitch until I get what the fuck I came for, and that's info on yo' brother." I could tell that she was nervous because her hands were shaking. I looked at Cannon, nodded my head, and he let off a shot that hit her wall. That caused her to duck, and I kicked that hoe right in her fuckin' face, causing her to drop the gun. Putting my gun to her head, I pushed her up against the wall.

"Where the fuck is your brother?" I gritted out.

"Fuck you!" She screamed.

"You not about this life, shorty, and this ain't your mutha-fuckin' fight. I'm not gone ask you again, I'll just kill yo' ass and go through yo' shit. I can almost bet that I will find what I'm looking for." I was tired of talking to this hoe.

"He lives out West. His address is 3908 Hillshire!" She was mad as hell, and just as I let her go, this bitch tried to go for her gun. I put two shots in her ass and walked out the house. I'm not playing with these bitches or niggas 'bout mine. It took us about twenty minutes to get to the address she gave us. We got out the car, I put my vest on and grabbed my muthafuckin' choppa.

"Yo, this shit looks abandoned," Cannon said as we walked up the steps and I kicked the door in.

"Yeah, it does, but we gone check the shit out anyway."

We searched the house and it was definitely abandoned. Once we checked every inch of this muthafucka, we left out.

"Fuckkkkkk! If I could go back and kill this bitch again, I would. Yo, check to see if there is any movement on his other sister," I asked Cannon, as we got back into the car.

"Jimmy said there hasn't been anybody there since we put them on the house," Cannon said.

"Fuck! Let's get to the warehouse and then we will figure this shit out." I was in so much fuckin' pain; this shit damn near took me to my knees. I popped a pain pill that I got from Cannon, 'cause the lil' bitch ass paramedic said he couldn't give me anything. It was all good. We wasn't into selling pills on the streets, but we damn sure could get our hands on them bitches if we needed it. I could feel the blood running down my arm.

"Yo, find a 24-hour pharmacy. I need to fix this shit up." Cannon nodded. A few minutes later, he pulled into a Walgreens and got out the car. I laid my head back on the seat, waiting for him to come back out with the shit I needed.

"Stay strong, Bear. I'm coming to get you, baby," I spoke out loud, praying she would feel me. When Cannon came walking out of the store, I got out of the car, pulling my shirt off.

"I got shit I thought you might need to clean it up. Bro, when we get Cas back, you gone have to go to the hospital. This shit looks bad, and I would hate to see yo' ass walking around with one arm and a nub. I mean, you gone still be my nigga, but get this shit checked out. You gone clean my damn car out too, bleeding all over my muthafuckin' seats," this nigga said and burst out laughing.

"Nigga, fuck you! You got a shirt or something in here that I can put on?" I finished cleaning and wrapping my arm up, just as Cannon handed me a shirt. It didn't take us long to get to the warehouse. When we walked in, Marlo ass was deader than a muthafucka, and Dom was going fuckin' crazy.

"You killed my fuckin' brother, you stupid bitch! You a pussy ass nigga for that shit! Yo' bitch ass lucky I'm tied down to this fuckin' chair. I would kill yo' ass for this shit!" He yelled out at Priest.

"Unchain him," Priest calmly told one of the guys, and Keisha ass just sat there crying. As soon as Dom was loose, he jumped up going after Priest. I knew this shit was about to be good, but I'mma need him to hurry up and beat this nigga ass. Priest put his gun on the table and didn't even give his ass time to swing. He hit that nigga so hard I felt that shit, and I wasn't even in the muthafuckin' fight. Dom swung, hitting Priest in the Jaw and that shit must have pissed my brother off, 'cause he beat the shit out of his ass. I have seen Priest fuck a nigga up before, but bro was giving this nigga that work.

"Who's the pussy now, nigga?!" He roared, slamming Dom head into the concrete over and over again. Kicking him in the head, he stopped and walked over to Keisha bitch ass.

"Unchain this hoe!" He yelled. As soon as they got the chains off, he gripped her up and threw her ass up against the table. I took a seat because this is the shit I have been waiting for since the day he married this bitch.

"I never knew that I could hate a muthafucka as much as I hate you! Bitches like you don't deserve to have children. You set out to kill your own flesh and blood, a little girl that was innocent in all of this. I would give my life in a heartbeat for the life of my daughter and my unborn child. Don't get it fucked up; Sasha is my muthafuckin' daughter and that shit will never change. I will never leave her, and I will never raise her to be a conniving, hateful bitch like you! I gave you years of my fuckin' life, being a good man to you, taking care of you, devoted and faithful to your hoe ass! You deserve everything I'm gone give yo' ass, fuckin' heartless bitch!" This nigga was so mad spit was flying from his mouth.

"It was the medicine. My mind isn't right. I'm sor–" She tried to speak, but he cut her ass off by kissing this bitch lips. I knew then that this nigga was losing his fuckin' mind.

"That was the kiss of death, bitch! Fuck everything about your worthless ass!" He roared, slamming a knife down into her chest.

"Argghhhhhhhh!" Keisha screamed as this nigga stabbed her repeatedly and then pulled his gun out, emptying the clip in her ass. The kiss of muthafuckin' death? This nigga was crazy for real.

"Torch these muthafuckas!" He spoke as he walked out of the warehouse, and we followed him out.

"Did you get anything on Cas?" Pop asked me.

"His sister gave me a fake address, but Cam is looking into

some shit for me. I'm not resting until I find her, but I'm going home to get cleaned up and fix up my damn arm. Cam sent me a text saying that he was about thirty minutes away," I told him.

"I will meet you at your house in about thirty minutes, I need to go change," Priest said. I felt bad for my brother because I knew this shit was eating him the hell up.

"Bruh, you can sit this one out if you need to. We got this." He wasn't in the right headspace to be on the streets with the shit we were about to get into.

"Nah, I'm not gone rest until we get Cas back. I will see you in thirty," he said and walked away.

"Let's go." Pulling into my driveway, Cam was already here waiting for us. We all dapped up and went inside the house. I ran upstairs and turned the shower on to get this shit cleaned up. Just as I was about to step in the shower, something sitting on the sink caught my damn eye. I picked the pregnancy test up and couldn't believe what I was seeing. Damn, my baby is having my fuckin' baby! A nigga done put his hands on my girl while she's carrying my baby. I made the shower quick, wrapping my shit up and packing my guns in my duffle. Just as I was walking out of the room, something that Cas said to me hit me like a ton of bricks. Pulling my phone out, I called Tiff up.

"Yo, nigga, what the fuck is going on? I've been calling your damn phone all damn night. Y'all niggas ain't show up for the damn party. I even stopped by your crib and nobody was there," Tiff went on and on.

"Somebody shot up my car and snatched Cas. That bitch you had with you that night Cas and I got into it, you know where she live at?" I asked her.

"Yeah, you think she had something to do with this shit?" Tiff questioned.

"I think Cas ex had something to do with it, but for some reason, the shit Cas was saying about her popped in my head. How I'm feeling right now, ain't nobody safe, and I'm not letting shit ride. That bitch popped up for a reason, and if she got something to do with it, I'm killing her ass on sight," I told her.

"I'm sending you her address now, and I will meet you there. If that bitch got something to do with it, I'm beating that ass, and then you can kill the hoe." Tiff and I ended the call, and she sent me the address.

Chapter Six

PRIEST

I had to come home and get this blood off me. Stepping into the shower, everything just hit me all at once. I can't even express the amount of anger I'm feeling. Sasha is my life, and the feeling of knowing that my baby doesn't have my blood flowing through her is doing a number on my ass. It felt as if someone just ripped my damn heart out of my chest.

"Fuccccckkkkkkkkkk!" I roared, as the tears fell from my eyes. Nothing could have prepared me for the shit that I was going through right now. It took me a few minutes to get myself together. I took my shower and stepped into my bedroom. Once I got dressed, I grabbed my keys and headed out the door. I needed to be out helping my brother find Cas. I had a few missed calls from Nas, and I called him back to see what was up.

"Bro, we left the house. Meet us at the address I sent to your phone," he said.

"Alright, I will be there soon." I ended the call and put the address in my GPS. By the time I got there, the guys were getting out of the cars.

"Who house is this?" I asked, just as Tiff walked up.

"A friend of Tiff's, but for some reason, the shit Cas said about her keeps popping into my mind," Nas explained.

"Y'all ready to do this shit?" Tiff asked, pulling the chamber back on her gun.

"Yeah, let's go."

Tiff walked up on the porch and rang the doorbell. We stood off to the side and waited for her friend to open the door.

"Who is it?" She asked.

"Janelle, it's Tiff, I need to talk to you for a minute." We could hear the locks turning, and the door opened.

"Tiff, it's after three in the morning, and my nigga is here sleep. What's up?" She asked her.

"Your man, I thought you and that nigga broke up?" Tiff asked her with a confused look. I knew then that Tiff was fuckin' this chick. My cousin didn't do niggas at all. She had one bad experience with a dude and her ass been fuckin' with women ever since.

"Tiff, I'm not about to do this shit with you right now. I let you taste this pussy, and that's all that it was. I never broke up with my dude. I just enjoy fucking and sucking on you whenever I get the chance to do it," Janelle said, and I knew Tiff was about to snap.

"Bitch, I will never be pressed over a hoe like you. You better curve that muthafuckin' mouth before I stick my fist in it," Tiff told her.

"Look, I'm busy. We can talk tomorrow," Janelle snapped, as she tried to close the door.

"Nah, we 'bout to talk about this shit right now. You ever heard of a nigga name Black?" Tiff questioned.

"Uhh...Nope, never heard of him. I gotta go. If you want to talk, we gone have to do that shit later," she said and closed the door. It was something about her that didn't sit right with me.

"Man, fuck all that! That bitch was straight-up lying and I'm not with the bullshit! I need to find my muthafuckin' girl, and this bitch knows something about that nigga." Nas kicked that hoe door in.

"What the fuck!" She screamed as Nas rushed her, gripping her ass up with his gun pressed to her head.

"Bitch, you better start talking or yo' mama gone have to do a closed casket on yo' hoe ass. My girl was right about you; something ain't right with yo' ass," Nas said. Pop, Cam, and I went to check out the rest of the house while they stayed upfront with her.

"Didn't she say that her nigga was here?" Pop asked.

"Yeah. So, if he was in here, the nigga heard the commotion and left or his bitch ass is still in here somewhere," I said to them as we walked back out front.

"Yo," Cam called out, pointing to the door by the kitchen.

"Let's go," Nas walked up. Tiff and Pop stayed upstairs watching this Janelle chick, while we went down in the basement of the house.

"If you move another fuckin' inch, I'm gone blow this bitch head off!" Black was standing there with his gun pointed on Cas.

"Nasss! Oh my God, you're alive!" Cas cried out. Seeing her condition, my damn blood was boiling. Cas was in bad shape. Her fuckin' eye was closed shut, she had bruises on her face, and her lips were swollen.

"I'm never leaving you, Bear. Nigga, there ain't a muthafucka in this fuckin' house that's gone stop me from getting to yo' ass tonight. I don't give a fuck about that gun yo' punk ass is holding. I'm gone fuck yo' whole life up in this bitch tonight. You put your muthafuckin' hands on my girl and did her dirty like that? Nahhhh, you might as well kill me, 'cause nigga, it's about to be a massacre in this bitch!" I knew my brother was pissed when the veins in his neck started to protrude, and his voice became calm yet deadly.

"Nigga, you doing all that punk ass talking, and I'm the one with the gun to her head. Coming in my shit talking about yo' girl. This my bitch, and she gone always be my bitch," Black said, and I was tired of listening and looking at this nigga.

"Yo, this nigga voice is irritating as fuck," I stated. All hell broke loose when I sent a shot into his arm, causing him to move. Cas hit his arm that he was holding the gun in, and a shot went off. Cas hit the floor. Not knowing if she was hit or not, Nas let his Nine's rip, lighting his ass up.

"Cas, you good? Were you hit?" Nas asked her.

"I'm in pain," she cried out, and he lifted her into his arms. I knew the pain was killing him, but he wanted to carry her out of here. Walking up the steps and into the living room, this Janelle chick was sitting on the couch in tears. I lifted my gun and silenced that hoe as we walked out of the house.

"Damn, y'all niggas is gangsta with yo' shit. I like this shit, but y'all should have let me beat her ass before you killed the hoe," Tiff said.

"Damn, you fine," Cannon said to Tiff as we headed to the cars.

"Nah, I'm good. I'm allergic to the nigga edition. Y'all niggas ain't nothing, but fuckin' trouble." She looked at Cannon with her face in a frown, and I could only laugh at they ass.

"Girl, I will change your muthafuckin' life, and them bitches fuckin' will be a thing of the past." Cannon smirked and smacked her on the ass.

We got into our cars and went to Jefferson Hospital because Nas refused to go to Temple Hospital. Cas wasn't shot, but she definitely had some brutal injuries, and Nas needed to be seen as well. I decided to call Zoey so that she could get Cas' mom down to the hospital.

"Hello," she whispered, and I'm sure she was sleeping.

"Hey, I need you and Ms. Crystal to come down to

Jefferson Hospital. We got Cas, but she's hurt pretty badly, and I know she's going to need her family with her," I told her.

"Ok. Are you okay?" She questioned.

"I'm as good as I'm going to get. I will see you when you get here." I was in a crazy mood. Zoey and I still had some shit we had to work through, and knowing that shit wasn't helping my mood.

"They took your brother and Cas straight back. Your brother is in pretty bad shape. That damn boy wouldn't let them separate him and Cas, so they're in the same room," Pop said as he sat down beside me.

"I can understand why. I'm glad he was so persistent in looking for her right away. God only knows what would have happened to Cas if we didn't get there when we did. I'm going to stay and make sure they're good and then I'm gone head out. I can't get this shit with my baby girl out of my mind." I looked over at my Pops.

"I know, son. I can't even process all that has happened right now. But know that I'm with you, nothing is going to change the way we feel about Sasha. That's your daughter and my granddaughter, and we will get through this together," Pop stated, just as Zoey, Eva, and Ms. Crystal came running into the hospital.

"How is she?" Zoey asked.

"We don't know right now. They're checking her and Nas out, and we should hear something soon. All we can tell you is that she was not in good shape, and you both need to be prepared for what you see when you go back there." I didn't want them to go back and see Cas without knowing what to expect.

"Oh my God." Ms. Crystal was in tears, and so was Zoey as she wrapped her arms around her aunt.

"Ladies, why don't you two have a seat? I will go check to see if we can go back and see them," Pop said, but I stopped Zoey before she could sit.

"Come walk outside with me, beautiful." Grabbing her arms, we walked outside.

"Are you ok?" I looked at her, because she was pregnant, and I needed her to take it easy.

"No, I need to know that she's going to be alright." I pulled her in for a hug.

"I know, but Cas is resilient, and I know she's going to be alright. I just need for you to take it easy. I know a lot of shit has happened, but promise that you will try not to stress and get some rest." I looked at her.

"I will do my best, but it's hard to do. Are you alright?" She asked.

"No, but there is no need to talk about me right now. Let's get back inside so that you can see Cassie," I said because I didn't want to discuss my issues with her right now.

Chapter Seven

CASSIE

I was in so much pain, I could barely move. I didn't think I was going to make it out of there alive. Black was a cruel, vindictive nigga, and I'm so glad his ass got exactly what he deserved.

"Shit!" I screamed, grabbing my stomach.

"What's wrong, babe?" Nas stood up.

"The pain in my stomach and face is killing me." Just as he was getting ready to respond, the doctor walked into the room.

"Hi Cassie, I'm Dr. Jackson. I'm sorry that this has happened to you. Besides your face, were you struck anywhere else?" Dr. Jackson asked.

"Doc, she's pregnant and complaining that her stomach is hurting. Can you check and make sure my baby is good?" Nas asked and I looked over at him.

"How do you know that?" I questioned.

"You took the test, Bear, and left it on the sink. That shit said you got my baby in you, and we need to make sure y'all good," Nas stated, sitting back down.

"I will run some tests to make sure you're alright," Dr. Jackson stated, checking my face and back out.

"It doesn't appear that anything is broken. However, you have a great deal of swelling and lacerations, but they will heal with time. I'll put in an order for tests and blood work so that we can make sure your baby is alright," he told me as he turned to check Nas out.

"Mr. Chamber, you're a very lucky man, we're going to get these wounds cleaned up for you, and get you sewn up. I'm going to give you some fluids as well and make sure they bring a bed in here for you. I'm not sure if you two will be able to go home tonight, I may want to keep you at least overnight. Let me get all of the results back, and I will have a definite answer for you," Dr. Jackson stated and walked out of the room.

A few minutes later, the nurse came in and drew blood from me. She told us that they should be bringing the bed in for Nasir soon. His ass was not budging about going into his own room.

"The only reason I'm not putting up a fight about going home is that I need to make sure you good, Bear. Other than that, I would've been taking my ass home to my bed." Nas smiled at me.

"I love you, Nasir. I was so fuckin' scared that you were dead. I never want to feel that type of pain again," I cried.

"Shhhhh, don't cry, baby. I'm never leaving you. When your mama said she saw somebody snatch you up, I knew it was that nigga. I didn't need proof, I just felt that shit, and I felt something was up with that bitch, Janelle. There was no way that I could live with myself if something happened to you." He bent down, kissing my swollen lips, and I was grateful for this man. The door opened, Zoey and my mom came walking into the room, and I just broke down right along with them. I thought I would never see them again, and that shit fucked with me. It has always been us, and to even think that I wouldn't ever see them again was a scary feeling.

"Cas, my God, I can't believe they did this to you. I'm so sorry, baby," my mom cried, holding me in her arms. I was so happy to see her.

"I love you, mom." I know that she was worried to death about me.

"I'm so happy to see you, sis. Not knowing where you were was hurtful, and I'm just so happy you're alright. I'm so relieved that you're ok. Nas, thank you so much for putting her first. I will forever be grateful to you for that." Zoe walked over, hugging him.

"I'm gone always put her first, that's my life right there. Ma, stop all that crying, she gone be straight." Nas looked over at my mom, smiling at her.

"Thank you. You said you would bring her home, and I

love you for protecting my child. How are you feeling, Nasir?" My mom asked.

"I'm gone be straight, ma. Stop thanking me. As her man, that's what I'm supposed to do."

Priest walked into the room. I know what kind of man I have, who was gone be ready for whatever, but I have a newfound respect for him because that nigga was impatient as hell when it came to killing a nigga. I've heard stories about him, but I saw firsthand tonight that his ass didn't play.

"How are you feeling, baby girl?" he asked as he walked up to the bed.

"In pain, but I'm going to be ok," I replied.

"That's good to know. I'm glad you both will be alright. I wanted to make sure that you both were good before I went home." Priest seemed like something was bothering him.

"Bro, you gone be good?" Nas asked.

"Yeah, one day at a time." Zoey looked over at him.

"Zoey, if you want to stay, Pop said he will drop you off." He smiled at her.

"Zoey, you can go with him. We will be fine." She looked exhausted so I wanted her to go be with Priest.

"Ok." She gave Nas and I a hug, and they both left. My mom said that she didn't want to leave us, so she would be here with Nas and I until they let us go home. Eva and Kash walked into the room, but everyone had to step out so they could get the bed into the room. The doctor came back into the room about twenty minutes later.

"Is it alright to speak freely, or do we need your guests to step out for a minute?" He asked.

"We're good," Nas told him.

"You are definitely pregnant. I will need to do an ultrasound to make sure the baby is alright and I will let you know how far along you are as well. Give us a few, and we will be back in to get everything done," he stated.

"Oh my God, I'm going to be a grandma!" My mom jumped up, hugging me.

"Congrats to the both of you," Eva stated.

"Thank you." I smiled.

"Man, you gone have this knucklehead's baby? I pray that the baby comes out acting like you, Cas," Kash laughed. I couldn't believe that Nas and I were having a baby. I wasn't even uneasy about it because I was looking at everything that happens in my life differently from this point on.

Chapter Eight

ZOEY

I t was a quiet ride on our way back to Priest's house. I wanted to say something to him, but every time I attempted to say something, but the words wouldn't come out. It was almost nine in the morning and I knew he had to be tired. Hell, I had just fallen asleep when he called saying we needed to get to the hospital. Pulling into his driveway, he got out of the car, walked around to my side of the car and opened the door. Neither of us said a word as we entered the house.

"Ms. Carol is off today, so I'm going to fix you some breakfast. Then I'm going to bed for a little while, I think you need to do the same," he spoke, as we walked into the kitchen.

"Are you eating with me?" I asked.

"I'm not hungry right now, but I need to make sure that you and my baby eat something. I'm almost certain you haven't eaten anything since you left New York yesterday." I couldn't even respond to him because he was right. I was planning on eating when I got to the club for Cas' party.

"Are you going to tell me what happened here last night? I pulled up, and your dad made me leave. I know some of the stories from what Kash and Big Mama told me, but something tells me it's much more to it." He looked over at me with a defeated look in his eyes.

"I rather not talk about any of that right now." He turned to finish cooking my food.

"Priest, you can talk to me. Tell me what's going on." I didn't want him to shut me out.

"Fuckkkk, Zoey! She's not my biological daughter!" He roared, and I jumped as he stared at me. I was ready to get up and walk out of here until I saw the condition he was in. Tears pooled in his eyes and began to fall, and my fuckin' heart broke into a million pieces. I moved to him as quickly as my legs could get me. Wrapping my arms around him and holding him tight is all I could do.

"I'm sorry, I didn't mean to yell at you. I'm just in a fucked-up mood, and I didn't mean to take it out on you."

"Priest, are you sure there isn't a mistake?" There has to be some kind of mix up.

"Yeah, I'm sure. I really don't want to talk about it anymore." Wiping his face, he turned to fix my plate. I just sat there in silence thinking about what he just told me. I can't even imagine what he's going through right now. Priest and I were going through our shit, but I know deep down that he's a good man, and he loves his daughter. He sat my breakfast down in front of me with eggs, bacon, and toast.

"I'm going to bed now; your room is exactly the way you left it. Enjoy your breakfast." He walked out of the kitchen, and I swear I didn't have an appetite. After I finished eating, I went up to my bedroom to take a shower. I was about to climb into bed but decided against it. I didn't bother putting on any clothes, because he loves to see me naked carrying his baby. As soon as I opened his door, I wanted to close it back and go back to my damn room. Seeing him lying in the middle of his bed with nothing on, did something to me.

I didn't want to sleep with him again until we worked some of our issues out. But if I was being honest with myself, he was all I wanted. Besides that, I'm a horny pregnant mess. Easing into his room, I climbed into his bed and cuddled up next to him in his arms. He closed his arms around me and pulled me closer, making me feel a sense of relief until we both drifted into a good sleep. I felt a strong sensation run through my body, and I couldn't control the feeling. It felt too good to be a dream. I opened my eyes, and Priest had my legs spread apart, sucking and licking on my pussy like it was the last one he was gone ever taste.

"Ahhhhh," I moaned, as I gripped my breast with one hand and wrapped my other hand around his head. I could feel my pussy throbbing in his mouth as he applied pressure to my clit. I couldn't control my cries of pleasure, and he never let up; he only went harder. There were no words between us. This man was doing a number on my pussy and I felt like I was going to explode.

"Give it to me, baby. I know you're ready to burst, and I want to taste every bit of this shit." I guess that was all I needed to hear because cum rushed out of my ass. I was so caught up in the feeling tears just flowed from my eyes.

"Ohhhh. Shit! It feels so fuckin' good!" I screamed as I tightened my thighs around his head. No matter what this man does to me, he brings out my emotional side. It was a deep connection that I just couldn't reach unless it was with him.

"I figured since been a few days and you needed that release. Let's take a shower so that I can feed my child's mother. And before you give me a long, drawn-out speech about us not being together, trust me I know. I need to feel some type of normalcy right now, and us not discussing the obvious would help me right now. If you don't want to shower with me, I can use the guest shower while you use mine." He looked over at me, and could tell that he was trying to be strong, but his spirits were broken. I could see it all in his face.

"I want to shower with you, your baby is up and would like to feel your touch." He gave me a small smile and lifted me from the bed, carrying me inside the bathroom. After our shower, we got dressed, because I wanted to check on Cas and Nas.

"Do you think Nas and Cas are still in the hospital?" They were both in pretty bad condition.

"Yeah, Pop called me while you were sleeping. He said that the doctor wanted to keep an eye on both of them for a couple of days. He also told me that Cassie is pregnant," he stated, walking into his closet.

"Cassie is pregnant? Oh my God! I told her she was pregnant." I was so damn happy for her and Nas.

"And so are you, so stop jumping up and down, making my damn baby dizzy." He smiled, kissing my lips as he grabbed my hand so we could leave out. We decided to go to the hospital, and then have dinner since it was a little after four. When we made it to the hospital, we signed in and headed up to the 4th floor. Walking into the room, Nas ass was in the bed with Cas, and my aunt Crystal was in a recliner stretched out.

"Man, what kind of arrangements have you made with this damn hospital? Aren't you supposed to be in your bed?" Priest asked.

"Yeah, but I wanted to lay next to my babies, so they let me climb in bed with Bear whenever I want to." Nas smiled, but he seemed a little weak.

"That's not how it went down. He told them that it was their fault that we were here because the doctor wouldn't let us go home. And he has made friends with all the nurses on the floor, this nigga bought all of them lunch from Bianca's. When he got a taste of the food they had in here, he went off. He called Ms. Carol first, and she told him she was off today. Then he called your dad, saying that he was a burger short from killing over from starvation. He didn't want anybody working on us that had to eat lunch from here. He said bad food makes you feel worthless and unappreciated. So, they cooked all this food down at Bianca's, brought it up here, and now the nurses love him. They come in here, checking on his ass every ten minutes or so. I'm in too much pain to even get an attitude or give a damn, and mom thinks it's the funniest shit ever," Cas said, and we all fell out laughing.

"Bear, you almost sound like a lil' hater, with yo' snitch ass," Nas said as he got out of bed with her, and crawled back into his bed.

"I'm so happy for you two, Cas we're going to be able to raise our babies together." I smiled.

"I know, I can't wait to meet my little munchkin and yours. It seems surreal, but I'm excited and grateful that my baby wasn't hurt in all the shit I went through with Black. Thank God they got me when they did; shit could have been much worse. Eventually, my bruises will heal, and I'm sure I will have a few scars for the rest of my life. But I can't tell you how grateful I am that God spared my life," she broke down and cried. I wrapped my arms around her and told her how much I loved her.

"It's going to be alright, baby. We are all going to be right here for you. I'm not going back home until the two of you are back to your normal selves," my aunt Crystal said.

"Dry those tears, babe. We gone be straight. I will never allow someone to get next to us like that again, I promise you that. All I want is for you to get better and experience the most beautiful thing a woman can, and that's bringing our baby into this world. That's all you got to do, I got everything else." Nas was exactly what Cas needed, and I'm truly happy that she has him.

"Ok, I just get so emotional thinking about it. I will feel much better when we go home. The doctor wants to monitor me for a little while, and they have to make sure his fever goes down, and his infection starts to clear up," she stated, and Priest looked over at his brother.

"Bear, they ass was fine believing that you were the reason we were still here. I swear we gone have to work on them lil' snitch tendencies yo' ass got in you." Nas shook his head, and Cassie couldn't help but laugh.

"I'm sorry, baby. I didn't know we were keeping it a secret." She shrugged.

"I would have done the same if it was Zoey and me in that position," Priest stated, and I looked over at him. Hearing him say that had me feeling mushy inside. I knew I wanted to forgive him, but I didn't want to rush my decision to move forward with him. It still hard to get that night out of my mind, and I never want to feel that way again. We spent a few more minutes with them, and we left to go have dinner.

Chapter Nine

KASH

I knew I needed to get out of this bed, but I was tired as hell with all the shit that my sons went through last night. I'm glad that everything worked out, and everyone is safe. It was hard to wrap my mind around what Keisha did to Priest. I can't believe that Sasha isn't his child. I can't even imagine how my son is feeling about that shit. Keisha ass had to die, and if he wasn't able to do it, I damn sure would have. And I would've enjoyed every moment of it.

"Babe, are you hungry?" Eva asked, walking into the room.

"I could eat something. How long have you been awake?" I asked her.

"I've been up for a few hours, trying to get some work done and helping your mom out with Sasha. Priest tried to come and get her, but your mom wouldn't let her go. She said they're staying with you for a few days."

"Yeah, she wants Priest to have a little time to himself, so he can get his mind right." I hope all of this shit doesn't have her rethinking being in a relationship with me. I know the average woman would have left by now.

"I'm praying for him. What that girl did was so fucked up. Your mom made dinner, and your plate is in the microwave. Would you like me to warm it up and bring up to you?" She asked.

"Nah, I'm going to jump in the shower and go downstairs to eat. I want to play with Sasha, and then I will be back up to play with your beautiful ass."

"I was planning to go home tonight, but I will stay if you want me to." She knew how I felt about her going home, but if that's what she wanted to do, I was cool with it.

"I'm good on whatever you would like to do." I got up to go into the bathroom. Once I was done with my shower, I walked into the bedroom, and Eva was gone, so I assumed she went home. Walking downstairs, I could hear my mom on the phone laughing her ass off.

"Who you on the phone with, woman?" I questioned, kissing her cheek.

"I'm talking to your crazy ass son. Let me go, boy, your father just came down. I will see you in the morning." My mom ended her call with Nas.

"I see Eva left. I thought she was staying here with you?" My mom looked over at me.

"No, she's not staying here, but I want her to move in with me. We're together, she's just not living here yet, but I'm not pressuring her on the issue," I told her, and my mom was sitting there with a weird-ass look on her face.

"Do you trust her? You don't think she's into them roots, do you? Because this family has been through enough mess. I would hate to have to pull my choppas and my bible out on the heifer, but I will." I burst out laughing at my crazy ass mama.

"Ma, you don't own no damn choppas. Where the hell you get that shit from?"

"That's what Nasir said. He was like *'ma, you pulled the choppas out on them niggas'*. Priest got plenty of guns in that room, he just gone have to go buy him some more or use what he got." She shrugged, and I shook my head.

"You need to go read your bible, 'cause the devil is trying to break through, and we can't have that." I laughed at her ass.

"I had to protect my family; the Lord will forgive me. I'm going to bed. I will see you in the morning." She walked out of the kitchen, and I decided to go back to bed. I was a little pissed that Eva walked out without saying goodbye.

———

The doorbell going off woke me out of my sleep. Looking over at my clock, it was almost noon. I must have been tired as hell. I got out of bed to go answer the door, but by the time I got downstairs, Ma had already answered it.

"Whose flowers are those?" I asked her.

"Oh, these are for Eva. That was nice of you. I think you

should have sent them to her house being as though she doesn't live here." She placed the flowers on the counter, and my blood began to boil.

"I didn't send her these shits," I said to her, snatching the card out of the flowers.

I had a good time last night, baby. XOXO. It read.

I was ready to fucking explode, but I had to calm down and find out what the fuck this was all about first. I ran upstairs, took care of my hygiene, and got dressed. On my way out the door, I grabbed the flowers off the counter and left the house. It took about twenty minutes to get to Eva's place. I rang the doorbell and waited for her to answer it.

"Kash, what are you doing here?" She asked.

"Do I need a reason to visit my woman?" I sat down at the bar and placing the flowers on the counter.

"You don't need a reason; I'm just surprised to see you that's all. These are nice, thank you for the flowers." She smiled as she admired them.

"They are nice, but they're not from me. They were delivered to my house for you not long ago, and I thought you should have them." She looked at me and then back to the flowers.

"Oh, who would send me flowers to your house?" She pulled the card and read it. Her body language changed quick; it was almost as if she was nervous about something.

"Who are they from?"

"I'm not sure. It doesn't have a name or anything on it." She smiled.

"What did it say?" I asked because I really wanted to see how she would answer the question. She slid the card over to me, but I didn't pick it up because I already knew what it said. Never looking away from her, she dropped her head. I guess she figured I already knew what the card said.

"Kash, I honestly don't know what this is all about. I came home, did some work, and went to bed. I'm in a committed relationship with you, and I wouldn't do anything to jeopardize that." I stood and walked around to her, pulling her into my arms.

"I believe you. Do you still feel like someone is watching you?" I wanted to get to the bottom of this shit.

"Yes, I felt that way last night coming home. Even when I got inside the house, I felt uneasy. Seeing those flowers and reading the card makes me believe that someone is definitely stalking me. I've been getting calls too, but they just hang up after I answer the phone," she cried, and that shit pissed me off.

"Go pack your clothes. I know you like being in your own space, but until we get to the bottom of this shit, you will be staying with me. After we figure this out, you can come back home if you want to." She walked off to get her things together. For some reason, that nigga she was fuckin' before me came to mind. If it was him that is fucking with her, he gone see me. I guess these pussy ass niggas really got it out for the Chamber family, but they have to know coming up against us, you will lose every muthafuckin' time.

Chapter Ten

NAS

ONE WEEK LATER

Cas and I came home a few days ago from the hospital. Shit with me was a little more serious than I thought. We were both recovering well and that was a good thing. My infection was under control, and all my wounds were healing. She's been kind of quiet and not saying much when I try to talk to her about what happened. That was weighing down on me hard, but I'm happy we came out on top. I know shit is not always gone be peaches and cream in this street shit. That's why I'm thinking that it's time for me to step out of the game. I have a kid on the way, and that changes a lot for me. I'm going to run it by Priest, and Pop to see what their thoughts are about it. I'm thinking we can let Cannon run the shit, and we continue to get our percentages.

"Nas, are you ok? I've been calling your name and it's like you're in a daze," Cas asked as she sat up in the bed. Her bruises were healing well, but I got pissed all over again seeing her like that.

"I'm good. I was just thinking about how things could have gone bad for us. We have a baby on the way, and I think it's time that I make some changes in my life. Maybe open up some more legitimate businesses and work my way out of the streets. I'm definitely gone make sure you get your business up and running." I definitely wanted her to make shit shake with her business.

"Hmmm, okay," Is all she said. I didn't want to question her being short with me, so I let the shit go and changed the subject.

"Priest and Cannon are coming over. I think we should throw some shit on the grill and kickback."

"Yeah, I talked to Zoey she said she was coming over with Priest. She's leaving tomorrow, so I want to spend some time with her before she goes back. I'm gonna call Tiff and let her know we're cooking. We wouldn't hear the end of it if we don't tell her." She was right about that shit; Tiff would definitely go off. Cannon is on Tiff's ass hard, and I know watching those two go at it. It is going to be funny as hell.

"I'm going to see if Mom can make some sides to go with what you're cooking on the grill." Cas climbed out of bed and walked out. I appreciate Ma Crystal for staying here, helping us out for a little while. It was almost four and I still needed to make sure we had everything we needed for the grill. I haven't had a barbecue or dinner at my house since I moved in here, so I guess I needed to break it in a little. I think we needed to have a little fun after all the shit we have been through. Maybe that will help Cas feel a little better.

My brother has been going through a lot, and I think he needed to be around his family for a while. I hate that he and Zoey aren't back together and I know that shit is bothering him. He missed out on a lot of her pregnancy, and the fact that she lives in New York isn't helping at all. After I got dressed, I went downstairs to see what the ladies had going on. What I heard stopped me in my tracks, so I just stood there and listened.

"Cas, you can't possibly blame him for what happened," Ma Crystal said to her.

"Ma, if he would have handled this shit back then, neither of us wouldn't have gone through this bullshit. I got kidnapped and nearly beat to death because he let shit slide and not gone after Black. Hell, he was almost killed, and that scares the hell out of me. I told him everything, and he promised he would take care of it. I'm pregnant now, but what if something else happens? I need to know that he can protect me and our child." I couldn't believe the shit I was hearing. I would do anything and kill any muthafucka I had to, to make sure they were safe. I get it; I should have been on top of the Black issue when she told me he was a problem for her.

But damn, I didn't know baby girl was feeling like that, making it seem that I'm some sucker ass nigga. I didn't say shit. I walked straight out, slamming the door behind me and went to the market. I didn't want to say the wrong shit, knowing I was pissed the fuck off, and I might hurt her feelings. As soon as I got down the street, my phone was going off, and it was Cas calling me. I ignored the call and turned my music up. It took me about an hour to get the things I needed and make it back home.

Priest called me and told me that he was already at the house. Pulling into my driveway, I saw that Cannon had made it to. When I walked into the house, everyone was in the kitchen talking.

"Babe, I called you three times, why didn't you pick up?" Cas questioned.

"I didn't see your calls," I told her and sat the shit down on the counter.

"I needed you to pick up some things that Mom needed, but it's cool Tiff is going to pick it up on her way here." She sounded as if she had an attitude, but right now, I didn't give a fuck. I was in my feelings about the shit she said, and the longer I stood there, the madder I got.

"Ma, can you get this meat ready to go on the grill for me?" I asked her.

"Yes, I'll take care of it, baby." Ma Crystal grabbed the meat out of the bags, and Priest, Cannon, and I walked out of the kitchen and headed outback.

"Nigga, what the hell is wrong with you? Yo' ass look like

you ready to fight a nigga," Cannon laughed, looking over at me.

"I'm fuckin' pissed, nigga! Before I left to go out to the store. I heard Cas telling her mom that she blames me for the shit that happened to her. She said I should have handled that nigga a while ago. I can agree with that shit, but her ass is in there talking that shit about not knowing if I can protect her and my damn baby. I'm not feeling that shit. I would go to war and die for her and my damn child. The fuck she talking 'bout," I explained.

"Damn, that's fucked up. I don't even know what to say about that." Cannon shook his head, sipping his drink.

"Maybe you need to sit down and talk to her, man. She went through some traumatic shit. If after you talk to her, and she still feels that way, I'm not sure what steps you can take to make her feel comfortable. I mean, that was someone from her past. It wasn't like it was someone that was gunning for you and went after her. Once the shit happened at the club, you were looking for him, so that you could protect her. I don't think it's fair to blame you for what he did. He fucked both of y'all up; you could have died because of that nigga." Priest was right. I guess I needed to talk to her and see where her head was at. If she doesn't believe that I can keep her safe, then I guess we gone have to figure something out. That shit got me feeling fucked up right now.

"What y'all out here talking about?" Tiff asked as she took a seat at the table.

"Damn, you got to walk yo' fine ass out here with them tight ass jeans on," Cannon said, licking his lips.

"Nigga, what would you have suggested I wear, if I can't wear these jeans?" She asked him.

"Nothing at all. You could have walked yo' fine ass in here butt ass naked, sat that pussy on my face and let me suck yo' ass dry. That's what the fuck I would have suggested and wanted. Oh yeah, that's an open invitation for whenever you ready. If that pussy starts throbbing while we're sitting here, just say the word. Fuck this nigga and his barbeque; we can get us a to-go plate." This nigga had Tiff ass squirming like she got a bad hit of dope. She jumped up quick as hell, running into the house that her ass knocked over my damn chair she was moving so fast. I ain't never seen her shook like that before. The shit was funny as hell.

"Yeah, she can run now, but I'mma get that ass later. The only thing her ass gone be sucking is my tongue and this muthafuckin' python." This nigga must have forgotten who the hell she was to us.

"Nigga, that's our fuckin' cousin. She ain't gone be sucking yo nasty crusty ass dick!" This nigga got me fucked up. I don't care about him getting with Tiff, but we don't want to hear what the fuck he gone do to our damn cousin.

"My bad, she got my ass ready to hang it all up and put a ring on it," he said, shaking his head. Cas, Zoey, and Tiff came walking outside with the meat ready to go on the grill. Cannon's ass stared at Tiff, and she did everything in her power to ignore his ass. Tiff fucked with girls, but my cousin was a bad muthafucka, I had to give her that shit. Growing up, niggas was always trying to get at her ass.

"Can I talk to you for a minute?" Cas asked, but I took the pan out of her hand, walking over to the grill.

"Are you alright, you're acting like I did something wrong?" She looked at me, and I just stared at her.

"You should be asking yourself that shit, Cas. You're the one that has a problem with me. I heard what the fuck you told your mama. I would die for you and my baby. Hell, if we're being honest, I almost did die for you. I damn sure wasn't blaming you for what that fuck nigga did. I was shot the fuck up and refused to go to the hospital because I needed to find you! So, don't come talking that shit about you don't feel safe with me. I can protect my family, but if you don't feel that way, then maybe we need to figure out our next move. I love you, lil' mama, but if you don't want to rock this shit out with me, you need to let me know that, and I can do what I need to do." I left her standing there and went back to take my seat. There was no need to go back and forth with her, making shit worse. She's the one with the problem, so I guess she will let me know her next move. I'm not gone lie, this shit got me tight as fuck, but I'm gone rock with whatever she wants to do.

Chapter Eleven

ZOEY

I've been back in New York for a few days now. Priest wasn't too happy about me coming back, but this is where I live now. He's going to have to understand that. I do plan on going back and forth until I have the baby. And the last couple of months of my pregnancy, he's going to stay here with me. I wanted the doctor that's been taking care of me to deliver our baby. Once the baby is born, we will go back to his house for at least a couple of months. I think our arrangement is good, but he's still not feeling it. I guess we will have to work out the rest when the time comes. Picking up my ringing phone, I saw that it was from a blocked number.

"Hello."

"I thought you were going to call me when you got back into the city?" He questioned.

"I had some things to take care of when I got back. I planned on calling you today." He was still pissed about what happened with him and Priest.

"Do you have plans today? I miss seeing you," he asked, and I stopped to think about what Priest said about Ty. I really liked him as a friend, so I didn't see anything wrong with hanging out. I will respect him enough not to bring him to the house, since Priest will be spending time here.

"Yeah, we can do that, just let me know where to meet you." He let out a sigh as if what I said bothered him. This is how shit is gonna go for right now, and if he wants to remain friends, he's going to have to deal with it.

"Let's go to Bronx BBQ's. I will meet you there in an hour." I agreed, and we ended the call. I got off the bed and went to get myself together so I could leave out. I was running a little late, and I texted Ty to let him know. I decided to call Cas and see how things were going with her and Nas. I can understand that she has concerns, but to come at Nas like that wasn't the move. I told her that she was wrong; she was going to have to apologize and talk to him.

"Hey, sis. How are things going with you?" She asked when she answered the call.

"I'm good. How is everything going with you and Nas?" I questioned.

"We haven't talked much about it; he's been out of the house a little more than usual. He has a guard that is outside of the house, and if I leave, they follow me. I feel so fuckin' bad for what I said, and now I have to find a way to fix it. I was just scared, and I know I shouldn't have blamed him." I felt bad that they were going through this mess.

"Cas, it will all get better. We both know he loves you," I replied.

"Yeah, I know. I'm going to sit down and talk to him about it and pray his stubborn ass listens. It sounds like you're in the car, where are you going?" She asked.

"I'm meeting Ty for lunch," I said.

"Ahhh, shit. Now you know if Priest finds out, it's gone be some shit. That nigga is already on one, you gone cause his ass to be a whole problem for you and Ty. I'm gone send a prayer up for you, boo, 'cause you damn sure gonna need it," she stated.

"Cas, it's not like I'm sleeping with him. We're only friends, and it's not against the law to have him as a friend." I'm not letting Priest dictate who I can and can't be friends with.

"Bihhhh, it's against the Law of Priest Chamber. That's the only law you need to be worried about," she laughed.

"I have to go. I will call you when I get back home." We said our goodbyes, and I headed into the restaurant. Ty was waiting in the lobby for me when I walked inside.

"Hey, sorry I'm running late." I smiled, and he pulled me in for a hug.

"No big deal." He shrugged and walked up to let the waitress know we were ready, and she immediately took us to our seat.

"So, what's been up with you? You look good. I see the baby is growing." He looked at me and smiled.

"Thank you. I had a family emergency, which caused me to stay in Philadelphia a little longer than I planned. What about you?" I looked over at him.

"Working, making sure my business is good. Listen, I'm still pissed about the fuck shit yo' baby daddy pulled, but I don't want it to come between us. I miss seeing and hanging out with you," Ty said.

"If you can't let what happened between you and my child's father go, then we can't be friends. To be honest, you made it seem like we were together, and we were just friends. That shit wasn't cool, and you shouldn't have done that. You wanted a reaction out of him, and that's what he gave you. I'm not going to sit here and say that what he did was right because it wasn't. I kind of want to keep peace with Priest right now." Nothing concerning Priest was up for debate.

"Hmmm, let's enjoy our lunch."

I'm not sure what the hell that meant, but as long as he understands how I feel, then we're good. Once our food arrived, we ate and talked about the baby and some things he had going on.

"Dang, we've been here for a couple of hours. It was nice catching up with you. Thank you for lunch." I smiled.

"No need to thank me, let's get out of here." We paid the check and he walked me to my car.

"Girl, you look like you're ready to pop," he laughed.

"Shit, I feel like it. I will be seven months in a couple weeks. It's almost time for my little one to come and I can't wait." Which reminded me that I had so much to do before the baby arrived.

"I'm happy for you, beautiful. I will call you a lil' later. Maybe we can hang out this weekend and see a movie." He opened the door for me, and I slid into the seat.

"That sounds good, just call me." He stood and watched me as I pulled off. As soon as I got on the highway, Priest was calling.

"Hello."

"Hey, beautiful. I was calling to check on you. I haven't talked to you all day, is everything good?" He asked.

"I'm good, just went to grab some lunch. Is everything ok with you? How is Sasha?" He was having a hard time coming to terms that Sasha wasn't his daughter. He even went to sit down and talk to the doctor to go over the test results with him. Keisha was Sasha's mother; Priest just wasn't her father. I was surprised that he wanted me to go with him, but I'm glad I did. He completely lost it when we got inside the car. It was so bad that I had to text Kash and have him meet us at the house.

"I'm taking it one day at a time. Sash is her happy little self as usual. She has this thing for cornbread and milk, some shit she got from Big Mama," he laughed, and it was good to hear that coming from him.

"That is funny because Big Mama got me eating it too. I'm going to be big as a house messing with her. She sends me recipes every day." We burst out laughing.

"Don't be feeding my baby all that junk. Don't make me hire a chef to cook for you. I'll know you're eating healthy if I do that." He sounded serious, and I'm definitely not trying to have that happen.

"I will watch what I eat, I promise," I sighed.

"I hear you. I will call you later, baby girl. I have to finish up this piece I'm working on," he stated. We talked for a few more minutes and ended our call.

Chapter Twelve

PRIEST

Not having Zoey with me was getting hard for me; I needed her. It was hard hearing her tell me that she wasn't ready to come back to me yet. I will apologize to her for as long as it takes, but I feel like she doesn't hear me. Picking up my phone, it was Cam calling me.

"Yeah."

"Yo, I was at this party the other night, and one of the niggas I know asked if I was interested in doing a job with him out in Philly. So, I asked him the details of the job, 'cause when his ass mentioned Philly, my antennas went up. He said his cousin had a problem with a nigga out in Philly, and he wanted the nigga dead. I told him I was down, but we both know I would never do a job like that for fifty racks. So, the nigga gave me the name of his cousin, and it's the nigga you wanted information on. And the nigga he wants dead is you. I need for you to tell me how you want to deal with that, 'cause that nigga gotta go, and the bitch ass cousin gotta go too." I knew I would have an issue with that nigga sooner or later.

"He can get it! Put someone on Zoey for me. I don't want her to know that she's being followed, but I need to know that she's safe. I was gone let the nigga live, but since he made the first move, he's a marked nigga, and I will handle him myself. I will let you know when I'm coming to the city, and we can get at the nigga then," I told Cam.

"I got you. I'm putting someone on your girl now. We got her on this end. You watch your back out there and call if you need me." We ended the call, and I called Nas to put him up on game.

"What's up, bro?" He answered the phone.

"I just got off the phone with Cam. He said the nigga Zoey was cool with put a hit on my head. I'm going to handle that shit. I just wanted you to know what the deal was," I revealed.

"Nigga, you know damn well I'm riding this shit out with you. The fuck I look like letting you handle this shit by your-self," Nas fussed, but I kind of wanted him to sit this shit out. He and Cas have been through some shit, and I think he needs to stay home with her.

"Nah, I'm good on that, you need to be home with Cas. I will have Cam with me; this is something that we can handle." I was serious about that I don't need him for this punk ass nigga.

"I will let you know. I can't say that I'm gone sit this out yet. I need to holler at Cam first. I will be over there in a minute. I just got off the phone with Big Mama, and she said Ms. Carol cooked some damn fried fish, shrimp, hush puppies, and coleslaw." This nigga hung up on me. I shook my head and walked downstairs to go check out this fish because that shit did sound good. Leave it to Nas greedy ass to know my menu before I do. Besides, I need to see my baby girl. She's become attached to her great grandmother, and I think it's because Big Ma was always feeding her ass. I heard talking coming from the kitchen, and Tiff was sitting at the table eating with Big Mama.

"What's up, cuz?" Tiff said as she fed her face.

"What the fuck are you eating?" I asked, looking at them. Even my baby was sucking on a bone, and that shit looked gross.

"Boy, you better go get you a plate. Carol put her whole damn body in these here pig feet. She got potatoes, onions, and gravy over a bed of rice, wheeeew chile," Big Mama said as she sucked the meat of the bone.

"She ain't lying, this shit good as hell," Tiff stood to put more food on her plate.

"I'm not eating that," I stated.

"Mr. Priest, I'm cooking for you now, sir," Carol said, and I felt better. I couldn't believe my baby was sitting there having the time of her life with that nasty ass looking shit. I made a mental note not to kiss her little ass until after she takes a bath and brushes her teeth. I got a kick out of watching her;

she was growing so fast. It pisses me off to know that she was born to a woman that didn't give a shit about her. I hate that she will one day grow up to find out the bullshit that her mother did to her, but I will protect her from that information for as long as I can.

I had to be in the office early as hell in the morning to finish up the orders I had, so after I eat dinner and play with Sash, I was going to bed. I think I'm going to head back to New York this weekend and surprise Zoey.

"Why the hell it smells like ass up in here?" Nas crazy-ass asked with his nose turned up.

"They nasty asses in here eating pig feet and got my baby eating that shit," I laughed.

"Y'all niggas told me that it was a fish fry session going on. And I want some damn fish, got my mouth watering and y'all niggas over here eating hog ass!" I fell out laughing because this nigga was crazy as hell.

"It's not ass, it's the feet, nigga," Tiff burst out laughing.

"Same difference, it all still smell like ass!" Nas said with his face still frowned up.

"Uncleeee," Sasha called out to Nas, holding up her bone she was sucking on. I think she wanted him to pick her up, but this nigga had his face frowned up at my baby.

"Uncle loves you, but I'm not messing with you when you got pig ass juice running down your lips. I'm Gucci on that, why y'all feeding her that shit anyway?" He looked over at Big Mama and she was tickled to death.

"That's some good eating. Y'all don't know what you missing. How is Cassie doing?" Big Mama asked.

"She good." He shrugged, and I knew he was still in his feelings. About an hour later, Ms. Carol was putting the food out for us to eat. Nas made plates to go, and he left out. I took Sasha up to bathe her and tuck her into bed. I called Zoey to say goodnight to her and then dozed off myself.

"Priest, how long will you be in the office today?" Dana, my store manager, asked as she walked into my office.

"I'm going to be here all day. I have a few people coming in today that need some pieces done, and I have to finish up the orders that I already have. How is the new girl doing that you hired?" I looked over at her, waiting for her to answer my question.

"She's good, but I think she has some personal issues that she's dealing with," she stated.

"I care about my employees, but please make sure that her issues don't become a problem for the business." I smiled at her.

"So, would you like to join me for dinner tonight? I know you've been working a lot, and it would be cool to relax and have a few drinks." I'm not sure if I wanted to mix business with pleasure.

"Let me get back to you on that," I replied.

"Alright, just let me know." She stood and walked out of my office. I knew she wanted to fuck me; she made it known right after I hired her to run this shop. My heart only beats for Zoey, and even though we're not together, I can't see myself fuckin' up my chances of getting back with her.

Chapter Thirteen

CASSIE

I wish I could take back what Nas overheard me say to my mom. I've been having nightmares and I'm afraid to even go outside. At first, I was angry, hurt, and pointed the blame for all of this at the wrong person. I'm the one that got involved with Black. The fucked-up decisions that I made could have gotten Nas and I killed. I knew Nas would fight to get me back if he was able to do that. It took my mama to get me straight, and I appreciate her for that.

Nas has really been staying to himself, going out, and coming home late. He barely even sleeps in the same room as me since the day he overheard what I said. I tried talking to him, but he brushed shit off, and nothing was really discussed. I was healing really well, and I'm so grateful for that. I have an appointment tomorrow for the first time to check on my baby. I'm excited and nervous about becoming a mother, but I was ready. I had been keeping myself busy by planning Zoey's baby shower, and setting up a maternity shoot for her, Priest, and Sasha. The maternity magazine wanted to do the shoot, so they could use some of the pictures, but that would be Zoey and Priest's decision. That was something that Priest insisted on doing for her as a surprise. I got out of bed in search of Nas. I thought maybe he would come upstairs when he walked into the house. Walking into the basement, he was lying on the couch watching television.

"I need to talk to you." I stood in front of him, but he just laid there for a minute, not saying anything. He sat up, turned the television off, and then looked up at me.

"What's up, everything good with you?" He asked.

"No, Nas, nothing is good. We need to talk about what I said and how you feel. I never meant to hurt your feelings, which is why I never came to you with it. I was angry and scared, but it's no excuse for blaming you. I trust that you will do everything in your power to protect us, and I truly can't blame anyone for this mess but me. I'm the one that got myself caught up with Black and his bullshit. I'm sorry for saying that. I love you and need you, baby. I don't want you mad at me anymore; we have a baby on the way." I cried, and he just stared at me.

"Cas, I love you and will always put you and my baby first. Don't ever second guess that shit again, you fucked me up with that shit. I'm a grown-ass man; I ain't never been scared of a nigga in my life. That nigga bleed and breathe the same air as I do. I'm not saying that a nigga can't touch me, because clearly, a nigga did. But I'm gone fight to the end for mine, and that's all I got to say on the shit." He stood, pulling me into his arms.

I felt a sense of relief come over me. I was able to breathe again. I love the relationship Nasir and I have. We're able to work out our problems and move forward in our relationship. I hope Zoey can get her shit together and figure out what she wants to do. Because playing in Priest's face is not something she should be doing. Now, if she's sure she doesn't want to fix the relationship with him, and she's moving on, that's one thing. But she's clearly still fuckin' Priest and spending her time with Ty. She knows damn well that Ty wants to be more than just friends with her ass, and to be honest, I don't trust the dude.

"Come here, baby. We need to make up for lost time, got my dick feeling like pussy fell off the face of the earth. I done beat my shit long enough, this muthafucka told me this morning he didn't like the way I was doing things, and he wanted his pussy back." We both fell out laughing as he began removing our clothes. He sat down on the couch and pulled me onto his lap, pulling me in for a kiss.

"I love you, girl." He began kissing and running his tongue all over my body and rubbing his fingers across my pussy. The sensation from his touch was driving my ass crazy, and my pussy was on fire.

"Shit, I need to feel this dick," I moaned as I lifted up and he placed his dick at my opening. Sliding down on his pipe had my ass feeling like I was a virgin, and it's only been a couple of weeks since we last fucked.

"Got damn, this pussy wet," he groaned as he started moving in and out of me. The way I was feeling as he beat my pussy up had my ass ready to scream, and I did just that.

"Ohhh, fuck!" I screamed, as I bounced on his dick. He grabbed my ass cheeks, spreading them apart and slammed me down on his dick.

"Fuckk, this pregnant pussy is the truth," he growled as I began cumming all over his ass. He lifted me up and placed me down on the couch with my ass in the air as he slid back inside of me and murdered the pussy.

"I'm about to cum again, babe! Fuck!" I moaned. I slid my fingers on my clit, massaging the hell out of it while he pounded my insides.

"Dammnnnn, let that shit go!" He roared as he shot loads of cum inside my ass. Eventually, we got ourselves together and grabbed our things and went up to our bedroom.

———

"Good morning, you two. I made breakfast," my mom said as Nas and I walked into the kitchen.

"Thanks, ma. I love having you around here. I think it's best that you just move to Philadelphia. It's too damn hot in Atlanta anyway. I don't know how you live down there with all that damn heat. And we need you here with us. Cas doesn't know how to take care of no baby. I'mma need a real baby professional to help her, and I'm not hiring no damn nanny. I would rather pay you to help take care of your grandbaby. The house is big enough for you to be comfortable here, and if you're not good with that, we can just build Cas a lil' two-bedroom on the grounds out back," this nigga said and burst out laughing.

"That's a damn lie! We will build that shit for you." I laughed, flicking my tongue at his ass.

"I will think about that, but I was just about to tell you two that I need to head back to Atlanta to go and check on my house. I will come back in time for Zoey's baby shower." I was so glad that she would really consider moving here with us and I'm so happy that Nas and I are back in a good space. Nas and I ate breakfast and then got ourselves together for my doctor's appointment. About an hour later, we were walking in the doctor's office.

"Hi, I'm Cassie Avery, and I'm here for my appointment," I said to the receptionist.

"Yes, ma'am, I need you to sign in. I will need your medical insurance, and I also need you to fill out this paperwork." She handed me the clipboard, and I gave her all that she requested from me. I'm glad Priest didn't cancel my health insurance, he did tell Nas that he was gonna have to start paying for it.

"Babe, have you started paying Priest for the health insurance on me?" I asked him.

"Hell, nawl! We gone have our baby for free, just like we gonna continue to eat for free. As soon as yo' mama leave, we gone have our ass back over there eating up all his shit." I burst out laughing because this nigga was not playing. I filled out my paperwork, and Nasir took it up to the desk. It took about twenty minutes before we were called to the back.

"Ms. Avery, the doctor is going to do an exam today, so we will need for you to undress and put this gown on." The nurse handed me the gown and stepped out of the room. About ten minutes later, the doctor walked into the room.

"Hello, I'm Dr. Blake, it's nice to meet you both. Ms. Avery, I'm going to do an examination and then we will take a look at your little one. Has everything been going well? I saw on your paperwork that you were recently hospitalized?" He asked.

"I'm doing much better, and I haven't had any real issues. It's hard to keep food down sometimes, and the vomiting can become a pain, but I know that's a part of the process," I told him.

"Yes, it is, but I can give you something to help you out with that. Let me get the nurse, and we will start your exam." He stepped out and came back into the room with the nurse from earlier. It took about ten minutes to do the exam, and Nas was watching his every move. I had to chuckle at his ass. For a minute, I thought his ass was going to fall out of the chair. He rubbed the gel on my stomach and started doing the ultrasound. The baby's heartbeat started going and I was in tears. When we heard the heartbeat at the hospital, I was the same way.

"Here is your baby," Dr. Blake stated, and Nas and I smiled at the sight of it all.

"Look at my lil' basketball player," Nas gleamed and I was gone let him have this one. If he wanted a boy, then that's what I hope he got. It doesn't matter to me what we have. Dr. Blake printed out some pictures and handed them to Nas.

"Ok, Cassie, it seems that you're roughly eleven weeks. I would like to see you back in the office next month. They can set your appointment up for you on your way out. Congratulations to you both." He shook our hands and walked out. I was so happy that my baby was alright, we went through some shit, but everything worked out for us.

"I love the beautiful faces you make when I'm deep stroking you." I kissed her lips as I thrust her insides.

"Mmmmmm, fuck me, Kash!" She cried out in pleasure as I slammed into her. Eva has no idea how good this shit really was. I pulled out of her and told her to come ride my shit. Laying on the bed, she crawled on top and eased down on my dick, rocking back and forth as she cupped her breasts in the palm of her hands. Grabbing her by her waist, I guided her up and down my dick as I punished the hell out of her ass.

"Kash!" She cried out, as we both released together.

"Baby, you got that good good between them damn thighs." I smiled, kissing her lips and then pulled her up, so we could shower.

"I can't even express what you have going on between your thighs." She shook her head, and I laughed.

"Girl, get yo' ass in this shower, and I can show you again just so you're clear." I winked at her. After we got dressed, we decided to do a little shopping. I wanted to pick up a few things for my grandchildren, especially for Zoey's upcoming baby shower. Eva said that she hasn't felt uneasy since she's been staying with me.

"Babe, I think I'm ready to give up my place and move in with you permanently." I looked at her because I was shocked to hear her say that.

"Are you serious?" I wanted her to be sure about her decision.

"Yes, I'm more than serious. I love being with you, and I love you. I don't want to be anywhere else. I'm in my happiest moments when I'm in your presence." She smiled, and that shit made me happy as hell to know that she was really in this with me.

"You just made me a happy man. I love you for trusting me with your heart. I promise to take care of it." I kissed her lips and we walked out the door, heading to the mall. Once we made it to King of Prussia Mall, we walked into Nordstrom's to do a little shopping. Walking out of the store, Eva stopped, and started looking around.

"What's wrong?" I asked her as I grabbed her hand.

"I have that feeling again like someone is watching me." She nervously looked around.

"Eva, I need you to be honest with me. Has this dude ever put his hands on you?" I asked her because the way she was reacting wasn't normal. She was scared out of her mind, and I know it's some shit that she's not telling me.

"No, he never did anything like that." I couldn't understand why she was so short right now.

"What has he done, or better yet what has anybody that you've been involved with done? Because baby girl, you're letting off some shit that I'm not too sure about. In order to help you, I need to know the full story about you. I don't need bits and pieces, because if some shit is coming my way, I need to know. It's not just me and you that I have to worry about and protect. I have my children, mother, and grandchildren to worry about. Let's get out of here and head back home; I can do this shit later. It's time for you to open your mouth and start talking. Don't bullshit me cause I'm good at picking out bullshit if I hear it." Grabbing our bags, I guided her out of the mall. It took about forty minutes to get back to my house. Placing the bags down, I walked to the bar and poured her a glass of wine.

"Tell me everything, Eva." I sat across from her and waited for her to start talking.

"To be honest with you, Harlem has never hit me, but he was an overly aggressive man. He would get angry if we had plans, and I was running late. Or if I was at work and I told him I was leaving the office at five, but I left at six. He was really angry when I told him that I didn't want to be in a relationship with him, but I ended up with you days later. He told me that I would regret my decision because men like you cheat, and men like him don't play games when it comes to his woman. I didn't understand his comment because I was never his woman. I did sleep with him, but after that, I kind of lost interest in him because all of my thoughts were on you. They were on you the first day I met you. I knew that I was attracted to you then. I didn't know if I would act on the attraction for you, but I knew that it was there. I knew what Harlem and I had talked about, so I didn't want to hurt his feelings." Tears fell from her eyes as she spoke.

"Do you really believe that someone is following you, and if so, do you believe that it's him?" I asked her.

"Yes, I believe that I'm being followed, and I believe that it's him. I've never had these problems before. This didn't start until I left him alone and got with you. The phone calls and the flowers with that crazy note lets me know that someone is watching me. How would they know to send it to your house?" She questioned.

"I guess you're right. Eva, I will make sure that you're safe at all times. I'm not one of these niggas to fuck with. I know you know who you lay next to every night." I've made no secrets about my past and what I was into back in the day. So, if that nigga wants to play, I'm gone play with him, but he won't be walking out of this shit alive.

Chapter Fifteen

NAS

Shit was back to normal in my house and I was glad. Priest and I were on our way down to Bianca's to see what was up with Pop. Once that nigga made sure we were good, his ass was back in pussy land. Big Mama getting tired of his ass, she ready to throw her hands and her mutha-fuckin' bible at his ass. Priest phone was ringing, and he answered the car speaker.

"Yeah," he answered.

"Yo, you not gone believe this bullshit. I put my guys on Zoey, and she's been hanging out with your boy. When I say hanging out, I mean for the last few days they've been together every day. Bruh, they have been out to the mall, lunch, dinner, all that good bullshit. And from what I'm told, she stayed the night at his house last night and is still there," Cam revealed and my ass was sitting here in disbelief.

"That's not a good look. I can't say that she knows what this nigga really got going on, but yeah you need to handle this shit asap," I said to my brother. I knew this nigga was pissed because his ass hasn't said a muthafuckin' thing yet. He made a u-turn and jumped on the highway.

"Yo, we on our way there. We will call you when we get close," I told Cam, and Priest ended the call. A few minutes later, he was calling somebody on the car phone.

"Hey," Zoey's voice came through the speakers.

"Hey, beautiful. How is your day going?" He asked her.

"It's going good. I haven't done anything, just lounged around. I may go out later. I have some things to pick up from the mall."

"Wasn't she just at the mall with bitch boy? How much shit can you possibly need from the mall?" I whispered, and Priest looked over at me. I guess he was telling me to shut the fuck up.

"Zoey, it's three in the afternoon, you need to get your day started. I need you to do me a favor. I think I left one of the tools I use to put my jewelry together in the bedroom I was sleeping in. Can you go check for me real quick and see if it's in there?" He asked her, and this nigga was officially a smooth ass nigga.

"I will go look after I take a shower. Can I call you back?" she asked.

"Yeah, take all the time you need, lil' mama," he said to her and ended the call. This shit was getting ready to get real ugly real fast.

"So, what's the deal with you and Zoe? I mean, are you guys working on getting back together?" I asked him because I'm hoping she has a reason to be hanging with another nigga. Well, let me rethink that. Because if me and Bear ain't together and she pregnant with my kid, the only dude she better be hanging with is God. That's the only friend she can have besides my ass. She will be walking her happy ass around the house singing what a friend we have in Jesus all damn day.

"I can't believe she would fuckin' lie!" Priest was pissed.

"Bruh, I don't think she lied. She just never told yo' ass what bed she was in, and whose shower she was 'bout to use. But we gone go to the real house that she's at and give that nigga the business, though," I laughed, 'cause this nigga was tight as hell up in this car.

"Nigga, sit back and shut the fuck up!" He yelled. I did what he said for now, only because I had to text Cas and tell her I will be home late. I damn sure wasn't gone tell her where we were going. 'Cause I know her lil' snitch ass would call Zoey and warn her.

———

We were ten minutes from New York, so I sent Cam a text to send us the address and meet us there.

"Yo, Cam just text and said that they left the house and they're at the theater. Ummmm, how the fuck are we supposed to kill a nigga in the movies, with a room full of witnesses? I'm a street nigga and I know we don't give a damn sometimes, but I ain't know dumb ass street nigga. I like my freedom, and my face is not made for channel 6, 12, 10, the jail report, or the mugshot department for NYPD central booking," I said, shaking my head. Cam sent the address, and I put it into the GPS. We were about twenty-five minutes away from Long Island. When we made it to the address, Cam and his guy were parked on the side of the theater.

"Sup, shit worked out in our favor. He's a nigga that rents the theater out for his privacy, but the manager is somebody that I use to fuck. She gone help us out, but I gotta fuck the hoe and give her some bread." Now I could get down with that shit. Priest popped his trunk, lifting the hidden compartment up to get his silencer. Once we got inside the theater, my ass got hungry. The smell of the popcorn had my ass in line order me some shit.

"Hi, what can I get for you?" The cashier asked.

"Let me get a large popcorn with some extra butter, and medium coke," I told her.

"Nigga, what the fuck are you doing?" Cam asked, laughing.

"The smell of this shit made me want some damn popcorn." I shrugged, grabbing my shit and following behind Cam and Priest.

"Cam, your guys can come around back to the exit door of that theater room. I've shut the cameras down and you should be alright. Make this the last time you ask me to do some shit like this, nigga." She stepped up to Cam kissing his lips and swayed her wide ass away.

"You niggas owe me. I hate when bitches kiss my lips and I don't know where they been," he fussed and open the door to the theater.

"I'mma stand back here and keep a lookout on this door," Cam told us.

"Nas, go that way and take a seat next to Zoe," Priest said, walking down the aisle.

"Yo, this is a private movie. You gotta get up outta here," bitch boy said as I took a seat next to Zoey.

"Nigga, sit your ass down and shut the fuck up! What up, Zoey? What y'all watching?" I asked her, but she was so nervous her ass was shaking. Priest took a seat next to bitch boy and the show really was 'bout to go down.

"The fuck!" Ty yelled, trying to go for his gun, but it was a lil' too late for that shit.

"Prie...Priest what are you doing? We were just out watching a movie," she stuttered. Trying to hold my gun, eat popcorn, and drink my damn soda became a task, but I managed to get the shit done.

"Zoey, get up and walk away now!" Priest roared, and my black ass jumped. The nigga scared my ass.

"No, what are you going to do to him? I'm not leaving, I will leave when you leave," she angrily spat, and I shook my head. He was trying to protect the fact that she was pregnant and didn't want her to see this, but I guess it's gone be what it's gone be, in this bitch today. I shrugged.

"Zoe, let me get them goobers since you not gone eat no more?" I asked her, but she ignored me and continued to look at Priest.

"Nigga, I'm not gone sit here and let you kill me! I told this nigga he needed to move on this shit," Ty snapped.

"Move on what?" Zoey questioned, Ty.

"Zoey, get yo' ass up and walk out with Nas!" Priest told her, and she still ignored him.

"Zoe, let's go." I stood and pulled her from the seat. She finally moved out of the row but kept her eyes on Priest and Ty. Priest did no talking to Ty, he sent two shots into his head and walked away. Zoey screamed and cried because of what happened to bitch boy.

"Zoe, I'm gone need you to calm down and stop all that damn screaming in my ear. He tried to get you to leave; you have no idea what's going on. Now get yourself together and act like you love me when we walk through these doors," I told her. If she knew like I knew she wouldn't be doing all that damn crying over that nigga.

We walked outside, and she showed me where her car was at. Priest ass was already in his car and pulled out of the parking lot like his ass was on fire. I drove Zoey's car back to her place because she needed time to get it together. It took us about fifteen minutes to get to her house, and Priest was already outside waiting. I knew it was getting ready to be some shit, so I decided to call Bear.

Chapter Sixteen

PRIEST

I was so fuckin' mad I felt like I was about to erupt right now! I can't believe this got damn girl was still fuckin' around with this nigga. I'm not sure if I'm falling for the, 'we were just friends' bullshit. But if I found out that her disrespectful ass fucked him, I'm done. There will be no working shit out because I tried with her.

"How could you do that shit? You killed a man because your fuckin' ass was jealous that I would rather spend my time with him than you! He's done nothing wrong but be a friend to me, and your thug ass murdered him! This is why I took my time about getting back with you. You're uncontrollable and I don't want to be around a nigga that has no regard for my life. Fuck you, Priest!" I could only look at this woman; the love I have for her is the reason I haven't wrapped my hands around her neck. I made a big mistake before, and I vowed to never jump to conclusions and treat her that way again. But to hear her talk to me the way she's doing right now was adding to the raging fire that was already building inside of me.

"Are you going to let me explain?" I asked her.

"No, I don't want to hear shit from you. I don't want a relationship with you. I will never keep my child from you, but the only thing between us is co-parenting our baby. I need you to leave. I can't do this shit with you," she said.

"Know who the fuck you're hanging around before you go to war for their ass, lil' mama. But I'm gone let you have this one! If co-parenting is what you want, that's what it will be. I will have my lawyer draw up financial support for you and the baby." I had nothing else to say to her.

"I don't need your fuckin' money; I have my own!" She yelled, and I kept moving. I don't feel bad about killing that nigga. It was either me or him, and I will always choose me and mine every time! I walked downstairs where Nas was, and we left out, heading back home.

"She really gone play shit out like that?" Nas asked in disbelief.

"Bruh, I'm tired of fighting. If this is what she wants, I will let her have it. Just as long as we make arrangements for our baby, she can do what she wants to do," I told him.

"Oh, you good, 'cause her pregnant ass would be doing that shit under my roof mad and all. Fuck that bitch made nigga. He had a hit out on your head. What the fuck was you supposed to do, let that nigga come for you? Nahhh, that's not how shit goes, and it will never go like that when the Chamber family is involved. Shit has been going bad with our family for the last couple of months because we let niggas and bitches try us for far too long."

Everything he said was the truth, but it's her right to feel the way she wants to feel. I will never beg a woman to be with me. I don't have to do that. Whoever is truly for me, will be for me. It was late when we made it back home. I was starving but didn't have an appetite to eat anything. After my shower, I crawled into my bed and went to sleep with Zoey on my mind.

———

"I got Sasha all ready for you. She's excited that she's going out with her daddy today." I decided that it was time that I gave Big Mama a break to go check on her house and see her friends. She keeps talking about this lil' boyfriend of hers getting upset that he can't see her. I know Big Mama is still in her prime, but she needs to slow down on that boyfriend shit. I had to smile because she was happy as hell to be going home. I loved having her around to keep me company. We've had some good talks, and I appreciate my grandmother.

"Are you ready for me to drop you off?" I asked.

"Yes, and your daddy is going to pick me up and bring me back here tomorrow. I think there is some leftovers in the fridge if you want to warm it up for y'all to have dinner tonight." I picked Sasha up and we walked out.

"I think I will pick up pizza for me, and this lil' beauty tonight." I smiled at my daughter.

"Pizzaaaa, yayyyy! Daddy, pizzaaa," Sash sang and clapped her hands, causing us to laugh.

"Your daddy done went and bought that girl all kinds of clothes. I still got stuff to hang up and put into her drawers when I get back. And she's going to spend the night over there next week. But I might have to rub her down with something to keep them roots off of her, just in case." I can't believe her ass was still on that.

"Big Mama, I'm convinced that Eva is a good person. You just got a problem with her because she got your son's attention. From what I heard, she's moved in, and he loves her." I laughed at the facial expression on her face.

"He told me she done moved in, 'cause she got some problems. I don't want my son in no more shit. This family has had enough problems," she fussed.

"Big Mama, you should know we're not going to let anything happen to her or him. He loves her, and to be honest, if she makes him happy, I'm all for it," I responded as I pulled in front of her house.

"I guess. I love y'all," she said as she got out the car.

"Bye-bye, Gramma." Sash waved at her grandma. I waited until she got into the house and pulled off. Sasha and I were sitting in Baskin and Robbins, and I heard a familiar voice calling my name.

"Priest! Hi Sasha," Dana spoke as she walked up to our table.

"Dana, it's good to see you." I smiled.

"Yeah, I was out doing some shopping and decided to get some ice cream. Do you mind if a share a table with you two?" She asked. I guess it wasn't going to hurt if she sat with us, but Sasha was looking at her all crazy.

"No, we don't mind. I was just waiting for my baby girl to finish her ice cream." She sat down, and we just had casual conversation. Once Sasha was done, it was time to go. I didn't feel like hanging with anybody, but my daughter. When Sasha and I made it back home, I let her run around and play in her playground outback while I looked over some numbers for my new store that was opening soon. About an hour later, I ordered a pizza and watched television with Sasha. I heard the alarm beep and knew someone was walking into the house. I knew that it was Nas or Pop, and it turned out to be both of them.

"What's up with you two?" I asked them.

"Just stopping by to see you and my granddaughter," Pop said as he picked Sasha up, tickling her.

"Have you heard from Zoe?" Nas questioned, and I truly didn't want to talk about Zoey.

"Nah, I don't think it's much for Zoey and me to talk about. I know when her next doctor's appointment is, and I know where it is. I will go up for the appointment, and after that, I will come back home." There was no need to push something that can't be fixed.

"I feel you. Cas has tried to call her, but she keeps telling her that she will call her back later and never does. Your pop got a problem with that lil' half-pint nigga that came into the restaurant putting claim on stepmama," Nas laughed.

"What's wrong?" I looked over at Pop, waiting for him to answer my question.

"He's stalking, Eva, and we can't seem to find the nigga. I put Cannon and Cam on him, and it's like the nigga went into hiding. But he keeps sending flowers to my fuckin' house, and I'm ready to kill this nigga. I called the florist, and they can't give me the name or information on the sender unless it's a court order." Damn, this shit is getting deep.

"Fuck a court order. If we make it a street order, them bitches gone talk," Nas said.

"The guys are looking into it for me, I know they will come back with something." Dad was right. Cannon and Cam would definitely get the information he needed.

"I'm here for whatever, just let me know," I told him, just as my phone started ringing and it was my aunt Shay calling. "Yeah," I answered the call and put it on speaker. "Priest this is your aunt, what have you done to my boys? Marlo told me they were coming to Philadelphia to get at you for what you and your ghetto ass brother did to them!" She yelled.

"Bitch, fuck yo bitch ass sons!" Nasir yelled out.

"That sounds like a YOU problem. We haven't seen your sons; make this the last time you call me." I hung up on her ass.

"Do you guys think she's going to be a problem?" Pop asked.

"Man, fuck her! I see why mom didn't fuck with her hating

ass. She can make noise about them niggas being missing all she wants, but she can't prove shit." Nas sipped his drink and I had to agree with him. Fuck her!

I got Sasha washed up, put her to bed, and went back downstairs to have a drink with Pop and my brother.

Zoey was gone make me fuck her ass up. I have called her over and over again and she's sitting her mad funky ass in NY watching the damn phone ring. Sending me to voicemail and shit, she got me mad as hell right now. She knows we don't do that shit. My mom went back to Atlanta yesterday and Nas and I miss the hell out of her. It didn't bother us one bit that she was here with us. I was praying that she really considered moving up here.

"Bear, why the hell you in here talking to yo'self and moving like you done got a bad hit of that shit? I'mma tell you now. I love you, but if yo' ass starts twitching, I'm gone drop you right off to friends on Roosevelt Blvd, so they can check yo' crazy ass out. I don't fuck with chicks that do drugs, and I don't fuck with chicks that got that different type of crazy running through they ass. I can do that hood crazy, but Nahhhh, I can't do that coo coo crazy. Mmmmm, mmmm, a nigga don't got time to be walking by, and yo" simple-minded ass is in a corner shaking and talking to yourself." I had to stop and look at this fool. His ass is the one that needs to go get checked out, crazy nigga.

"I'm about to go to New York and curse this girl out. I'm staying the night 'cause I know I'm not driving back tonight." I wanted to be there for her if she needed me.

"You need me to go with you?" I would have loved for him to drive me, but I think this needed to be a moment for Zoey and me.

"Babe, I think I need to go alone. She may feel better if it's just us," I told him.

"Ok, well, I'm going to stay over at Priest's house until you come back. I don't like how this house makes all these damn noises when I'm here by myself." I looked at his ass, and I knew why he was staying at Priest's house before we got together.

"Nasirrrr, you're scared to stay by yourself?" I asked him.

"Who scared? I ain't scared of shit. I just don't like being here by myself; I like having family around. Girl, I'mma thug, the fuck I look like being scared? A nigga run up in here, his ass won't be running out." I was crying laughing 'cause he can say what he wants to say, but I think his ass is scared to stay by himself, but maybe I'm wrong.

"Alright, babe, I'm about to leave I will see you sometime

tomorrow. But I will call you when I make it to Zoey's." He grabbed my bags and walked me out to the car.

———

By the time I pulled up in front of Zoe's house, it was a little after one in the afternoon. I grabbed my bags and used my key to get inside the house. Walking upstairs, I could hear the television playing, and I opened her bedroom door.

"Cas, why are you here?" She asked and I almost cursed her ass out.

"I'm here because your ass act like you can't answer the damn phone. Sending me to voicemail, like I don't know you're avoiding talking to my ass." This heifer got me hot.

"I don't feel like talking about it. He killed my friend and is trying to run my damn life. Ty didn't do anything to him, and your dude felt the need to take the shit for a joke. So, no, I didn't want to talk, just for you to tell him what I said." I dropped my bags to the floor because obviously this chick done lost her fuckin' mind.

"Let me tell you something before you make me go all the way in, on your ass. First of all, we're fuckin' family, and I will never tell your private business. Fuck that, I'm your sister, and you better get yo' shit together real quick up in here. When we started doing this shit, Zoe? I will always be in your corner and be here for you when you need me. You're sitting here going off because you're mad because that pussy ass nigga is dead. You're taking up for a nigga that put a hit out on your baby daddy! Hell, you straight-sided with the nigga, and had no regard as to why Priest moved the way he did. No matter if you thought it was jealousy, I'm here to tell you Priest did what he did because that shit was necessary. Where is the loyalty, sis to the man you've known longer? To the man that would move fuckin' mountains for you? To the man that loves your dirty ass drawers? To the man that has shown you how sorry he is for what he did? To the man that breathes your existence?

You're carrying his child, where is the loyalty, sis? Because for the life of me, I can't understand why you're so deeply connected to a nigga that put a hit on your child's father. Yeah, I believe that kill was mixed with a statement to let you know that he's not playing with you. But this is a dog eat dog muthafuckin' world, and I'm glad Priest put a bullet to his bitch ass head, because Ty was damn sure gone have one put into Priest's head. And if all else failed, he had you for leverage. Now I'm gone go take me a damn shower because you done pissed me off." I picked my shit up and left her sitting there in her tears and thoughts. I needed to calm down because I wanted to go back in there and go off again. I know as women we have our moments; hell, I just had a moment, but I had to get my shit together and apologize to my man. I called Nas to let him know that I made it and jumped into the shower. Once I was dressed in some comfortable clothing, I decided to lay in my bed. I heard a knock at the door, and Zoey walked inside.

"I'm sorry, Cas. I didn't mean to hurt your feelings. I didn't know that he was trying to hurt Priest. I'm so sorry! I said some horrible shit to him!" She cried, and I stood to comfort her.

"Let's just work on you right now. Priest will come around, and you two can sit down to really have a meaningful conversation. If you don't want to be with him, Zoey, you truly don't have to be with him. People co-parent all the time, just as long as it's healthy co-parenting. But I know that that man loves you and I know that he's sorry. Believe me, if I felt like he was on some bullshit, I would be the first one to tell him to suck a dick. And another thing, I'm gone always rock with you the long way. Don't ever talk that shit about me telling Nas some shit. Now let's go downstairs and order us some take out," I told her.

"Ok, I'm so fuckin' mad at myself for not listening to him. I thought Ty was genuinely my friend." She wiped the tears from her face.

"Sis, he was a street nigga; Priest embarrassed his ass. On top of that, Ty wanted your ass. He was capping your ass until you gave him the pussy. And what the hell are you doing staying the night at that nigga's house?" I asked her.

"How did you know that? I was just too tired to drive home after we ate dinner and watched a couple of' movies. I slept in the guest room; we honestly haven't done anything," she explained.

"I know because you're having a baby by Priest Chamber, the minute he got the call that Ty put a price on his head. Priest had somebody watching you and his unborn child. He immediately wanted you protected, and that, sis, is what you call love." We went downstairs to order some take out and relax. I hate I had to talk to her like that, but she needed to hear all that I had to say. I hope that Zoey and Priest can work this out so that they can get ready for the arrival of their baby. They both deserved to be happy and together.

Chapter Eighteen

ZOEY

ONE MONTH LATER

I have cried so many tears because of how I treated Priest. He won't even discuss what happened when I talk to him on the phone. If I call, he will answer, but it's only to make sure that I was okay. When I made it to my doctor's appointment last week, he was sitting in the waiting area when I walked in. Of course, he told me he was coming to the appointment, I just assumed he would pick me up. But when I texted him, he said he would meet me there. It was like he was nice to me but trying to avoid me at the same time. I apologized to him, and he accepted my apology, but then changed the subject back to the baby. My doorbell was sounding off, and I got up from the couch to go answer it.

"Hi, I have a package for Zoey Matthews." I signed for

the package and he handed it to me and left. The package was from an attorney's office. I opened it and couldn't believe what the hell I was reading. Documents where Priest has agreed to pay child support of fifty thousand dollars per month, and a trust fund for ten million has been set up for the baby, and an undisclosed amount will be deposited into the account each year. There was a two-million-dollar limit to buy a home in the state of New Jersey or Pennsylvania. The cost of all medical coverage and a nanny for the baby will be provided by him as well. I was sitting here in tears again; I can't believe he's doing all of this. My phone was ringing, I went to grab it and it was Cas calling.

"Hello." I tried to contain myself, but I couldn't stop the tears.

"Zoey, I was calling to see if you have left yet. Wait... Are you crying? What's the matter?" She asked.

"Cas, I just got the paperwork from Priest's lawyer. You should see all the things that he's providing." I read all of the documents to her, and we were both in disbelief.

"Damn, now that's a rich nigga taking care of his child," Cas stated.

"I don't know what to say, but I'm about to get myself together and get on the road," I told her.

"Ok, I should be at Priest's house by the time you get there. Be careful on the road, and I will see you soon." We ended the call, and I went to grab my bags.

My baby shower is this weekend. I was going to stay with Cas and Nas, but I wanted to spend time with Sasha, so I will be staying a week at Priest's house. I'm glad I left when I did because traffic is always crazy on Friday's. It took me a couple of hours to get to Priest's house. Pulling into the driveway, I saw him standing outside talking to this woman, and when he hugged her, my heart began beating fast as hell.

Did he move on? Is that his girlfriend? I thought. She got into her car and backed out beside me. I couldn't even get out of the car I was so caught up in my thoughts. I didn't realize that he had opened my car door.

"Zoey, do you have anything in the trunk?" He asked me.

"Yes, my bags are in there." I popped the trunk for him and got out of the car.

"Are you okay?" He asked as we walked into the house.

"Yes, I'm fine, just a little tired. It's been a while since I've been here, I see you changed up the furniture in here." I smiled.

"Yeah, I wanted to make a few changes. Your bedroom is ready for you and Sasha has been saying her mommy's coming all morning. I don't think you will be able to get rid of her this week," he chuckled.

"I wouldn't have it any other way. I got your paperwork from your lawyer; I think we may need to discuss it."

"Nahhh, we don't need to discuss it, unless you think the numbers are unfair. Other than that, I would prefer to leave it the way it is. Let me get your bags upstairs, and I will let you get comfortable. Ms. Carol is making all of your favorite dishes for lunch and dinner today." He walked into the room and placed my bags on the bed. I wanted so badly to ask him who the girl was, but I decided against it. My heart was indeed crushed to see him hug her. Once I got situated, I was off to find the little highlight of my life.

"Sashhhaaaa!" I called out to her, and she jumped right off of Big Mama and ran straight into my arms.

"Mommie, Mommie." She clapped, jumping up and down.

"Hunny, this has been all morning. It's good to see you, baby. Look at how beautiful you are. Pregnancy looks good on you, chile. When I was pregnant with Kashas, that damn boy did my ass dirty. I looked like I swallowed a damn bus. Hell, I think I still got some baby weight I need to lose." I burst out laughing because she was serious.

"Thank you, did she eat lunch yet?" I asked as I kissed Sash on her cheeks.

"Not yet, we were waiting on you to get here," Big Mama stated as we went downstairs to have lunch.

"Ms. Zoey, don't you look beautiful. It's almost time, are you ready for the baby to get here?" Ms. Carol asked.

"I'm more than ready to meet my sweet baby." It was hard to believe that this was really happening. I was going to have a baby. I try not to think about the times when I miscarried, but it was constantly on my mind. I prayed that it didn't happen this time. Cas, Tiff, and Nas walked in just in time for lunch.

"Hey, Zoe. It's good to see you," Nas spoke. The last time we saw each other it wasn't so good.

"Hey, Nas." I smiled at him.

"Heifer, didn't I tell your ass to call me when you were on your way?" Tiff said as she sat down in the seat next to me.

"My bad, boo. I forgot to call you. I was in a zone trying to get here to see my lil' boo thang." I pinched Sasha's cheeks, and she just giggled as she sat in my lap, rubbing my belly. Priest came into the kitchen dressed in different clothing, I guess he was leaving.

"You ready, bro?" He asked Nas.

"Yeah, let's go," he told him, and I was kind of shocked that he would leave when I just got here.

"You're leaving?" I questioned as he walked over to kiss Sash.

"Yes, I have some runs to make. Are you ok? Is it something you need me to do?" He asked me.

"No, I just thought...Nevermind, have fun." I know my attitude was showing, but so what. He picked Sash up and placed her into her chair, grabbing my hand and pulling me out of the room. When we made it into the hallway, he pinned me against the wall.

"Where I go and what I do, no longer concerns you. I will always be respectful to you because I have love for you, and you're the mother of my child. But just so we're clear, YOU set the stage for this show, baby. I think you said the only thing between us was co-parenting. This, baby girl, is what co-parenting feels like," he said to me and walked away. The tears fell from my eyes and I had truly fucked up. Once I cleaned my face, I went back to join the ladies in the kitchen.

Chapter Nineteen

NAS

Priest and I were on our way to meet up with Pop and see what was going on with him. He's been on one since they found the address that ole dude was using. When they got there, it was his mother's address. She said that she had been getting mail for him but hasn't seen him in a couple of years. Pop was pissed because we knew this nigga was gone try some shit.

"What's up with you and Zoe?" I asked my brother. I knew he loved her, but he was not feeling the way she did him.

"I'm giving her what she wants, and I guess she's not liking our co-parenting arrangement. If she needs something, I'm there. If she's sick, I'm there. I will do whatever she needs to make her feel comfortable until she has the baby. She made her decision to not be with me, so her getting access to what I have going on is over."

"Bruh, I honestly think that she was scared, and she looked at dude as a real friend. She assumed that you were acting out of jealousy more than an act of protection. She didn't know what he was up to, and I believe that if she did know, she would have cut shit off with him. She's pregnant and emotional right now. This is the time for both of you to sit down and put it all on the table. Be honest, can you really see another nigga raising your baby? Because if you're not gone be there with her, another nigga will. Now that some real shit for your ass to digest. I think you two have been through enough heartbreak, and it's time to get right." I hope he listens to what I had to say, 'cause I practice that shit all last night. I promised Cas that I would talk to his ass. I never had to give good relationship advice before. I would just go drag her ass home, and that would be the end of that.

"It is what it is." He shrugged, and we got out of the car heading into Bianca's.

"Lonnie, my nigga, I need me some wings, fries, and a beer. Priest, you want something?" I asked him.

"I'll take the same thing he's having," he told Lonnie.

"Pop, you know we're eating that shit for free, we kind of tight right now. We got babies on the way, and this nigga got child support to pay." I pointed at Priest, and we all laughed.

"What's up?" Pop dapped us up and we all sat at the bar.

"We just came to check on you. I know you've been

staying close to home, how is Eva doing?" Priest questioned, just as Lonnie put our drinks on the counter.

"She's hanging in there, but this nigga is really trying my fuckin' patience. The flowers stopped coming, and she was happy about that. But it wasn't because of his ass, it was because I told them to stop delivering the shit to my house," he spoke, and I could understand how he was feeling.

"Damn, that's fucked up. These niggas always want to do dumb shit and then hide their hand." I felt bad because I think we were all tired of niggas trying to come for us. I got to give to the lil' quart-size nigga, he was definitely on some bullshit with this one. We hung out with Pop for a couple of hours and then headed back to the house. Cas and Tiff were out back with the decorators going over how they would set things up for Zoey's shower. Priest spared no expense to make the day enjoyable for her. He said that she has gone through a lot and wanted her to enjoy the moment.

"How did it go?" Cas asked as she walked up, wrapping her arms around my neck.

"I don't know, you know that nigga is hard to crack. I think they gone have to work this out on their own. But I think after the shower tomorrow, we should bring Big Mama and Sash over to our house. That way the two of them will have the house to themselves. If that shit doesn't work, then we just lock they ass in a room, and they can't come out until they fuck." I shrugged.

"Babe, that shit ain't gone work," she laughed.

"Why not? That shit gets me all the time? I mean, the

apology is cool, but every time you get on this dick, I can feel how sorry you are. That shit works every time." She looked at me and fell out laughing.

"Boy, I swear you need a check, but if you say it will work, we gone try it," she stated, shaking her head.

"Tiff, I thought you would have left by now," I said, walking up to stand next to her.

"Hell nawl! We're having a seafood boil tonight. I'm gone sit my ass right here until I'm having trouble moving away from the table." I knew her ass was serious, and I will be right there with her.

"This is the best place on earth when it comes to eating a good ass meal. Ms. Carol's birthday next week, Priest and I got this nice ass gift for her." I couldn't wait to give it to her. She's gonna be happy as hell when she sees what we got her. Cas said that Zoey was upstairs taking a nap until dinner. Pop and Eva came over, and we all hung out and ate good.

Chapter Twenty

KASH

"I had a good time tonight at Priest's house. Zoey looks as if she is ready to pop. She's so beautiful, and I know they're going to have such an adorable baby. And Sasha loves her to death. I couldn't believe she wouldn't go to her dad," Eva spoke.

"Yeah, Sash loves her, and Priest always has a hard time when Zoey is around. I think it's cute, I just want them to work this shit out. My son has been through some shit, and I would love to see him happy. I know that Zoey is the only woman that's going to do that for them. Nas said they have a plan, so I hope the shit works," I said as we pulled into her driveway. Eva had some more things that she needed to pick up before we headed home. There are some things that we have to work on in the house, and then she's putting up for sale.

"Nas is the funniest; he and Cas are so good for each other." She smiled as I unlocked the door and walked inside. It was dark, and I almost tripped on something, I pulled out my phone so that I could have some light to see. When I turned the lights on, we couldn't believe this shit.

"What the fuck!" I yelled. This girl's house was fuckin' destroyed, shit was thrown all over the place. Her television was pulled off the wall. I mean, everything was destroyed. I pulled my gun out, and we moved to the back of the house. Eva was in tears, and I wish I could protect my baby from seeing this bullshit.

"Kash, he did this! I don't know anybody that would do this to me!" She cried. I just pulled her into me and let her cry it all out. Her bedroom was in the same shape, this nigga had gone so far as to take all of her panties with him. I'm going to kill this bitch nigga when I get his ass.

"I'm going to take care of it, baby, come on let me get you home." We walked out, and I sent Cannon a message that we needed to find this nigga by any means necessary. His mother said she hasn't seen him in years, but for some reason, I don't believe her ass. We made it home, and Eva decided to take a shower and go to bed. I was too fuckin' pissed off to sleep, so I had a few drinks to calm down so I could get some rest. We had an eventful day planned tomorrow, and I think we both needed to be around family right now. Now that Eva and I have moved in together, we're supposed to set something up for me to meet her mother soon. Eva jumped when I climbed into bed with her. I hated this shit for her.

"Eva, baby, you have nothing to be afraid of, I promise you I will always protect you." I needed her to understand that.

"I know you will. It's just so scary to know that he would do this to me," she cried. I pulled her closer to me and held her all night. I loved the hell out of this woman, and I would give my life to keep her safe.

The next morning, I got up and decided to make breakfast for Eva. We still have gifts to wrap for the baby shower, and I was definitely leaving that for her to do. By the time I was done with breakfast, Eva was walking into the kitchen and didn't have any clothes on. I swear I have never fucked a woman as much as I slide up in her ass, not even Bianca.

"Morning, Babe." She smiled.

"You damn right it's a good morning." I walked over to her, lifting her ass up and carrying her back up the stairs.

"What about our food?"

"Man, fuck that food. I'm about to eat right now and will feed you when I'm done." I trailed kisses down her chest, latching onto her breast as I slid my fingers over her clit. A moan escaped her mouth, and that shit was like music to my ears. I loved to hear the sounds of ecstasy escape her beautiful ass lips.

"Kash, my Godddd!" She cried out in pleasure as I applied pressure to her clit. I worked my tongue down her body until I reached her center, sliding my tongue across her pearl.

"Fuckkkk!" She groaned as I latched on. I sucked her pussy until she screamed my name, and even then, I still didn't want to let go.

"Damn, this pussy taste good!" I growled as I felt her clit pulsate against my tongue. She wrapped her hand around my head, pulling me closer.

"Shit, I need your dick in me, baby," she moaned, and I gave her everything she was looking for. I slammed inside of her, pulling my dick out only leaving the tip in, pounding in and out of her pussy.

"Got damn, I can't get enough of this good ass pussy. Fuckkkk!" I roared. Her pussy gripped my dick and sucked the cum and my soul right out of my ass as we both released together.

"Let's take a shower; you have gifts to wrap." I kissed her lips, and we got out of bed so that we could get our day going.

Chapter Twenty-One

PRIEST

Things were full speed ahead here because we had Zoey's maternity shoot going on right now. I can't believe that the maternity line she was contracted with sent these people here to do all of this, just as long as we permitted them to post some of the photos in the magazine. Zoey looked absolutely amazing, and she was definitely a natural at this. I could tell she was very comfortable with the people she was working with; she was in her element.

"Ok, Zoe, are you ready for your family now?" The photographer asked.

"Priest, where is Sash? I would like to take some with her first?" She questioned but I had no idea where she was.

"She's right here!" Cas yelled out as she walked into the room with Sasha. My baby girl looked so adorable. Zoey had on a beautiful beige gown by Christian Dior, and Sasha was wearing a dress by Baby Dior in the same color as, Zoe. Sasha laid on her chest as Zoey kissed her forehead, and they snapped the pictures. That moment will forever be etched into my mind. My baby seemed so comfortable and the love they both had for one another was evident.

"Priest, are you ready?" I didn't even realize she was calling my name; I had zoned out.

"Yes." When she slid the straps off of her shoulders and her dress pooled around her feet, I was stuck. This woman was absolutely beautiful, the artwork on her body was dope as hell.

"Sir, you're going to have to lose the shirt," the girl that was helping Zoey said to me, and Zoe chuckled. I did as I was told and removed my shirt, and the photographer started taking shots of Zoey and me. I think the photo of me kissing her stomach was a meaningful shot because I did that to her every chance I got.

"You guys did great. Zoey, we will send the photos over to you later today. Priest, it was nice meeting you," the photographer stated, and they said their goodbyes to Cas and Zoey.

"Priest, you did good. Thank you for thinking of this for me." She smiled and walked away. Things between us were awkward, and I didn't want it to be that way. The doorbell was ringing, and when I opened the door, it was Dana.

"Hey, I know you wanted me to drop this off to you tomorrow. But something came up, and I wanted to get it over to you," she stated, just as Zoey walked out of the kitchen. She looked at Dana and walked upstairs without speaking, I tried calling out to her, but she kept walking.

"Thanks for dropping this off." I opened the door, and she left. I had an hour to get dressed before everyone arrived. Once I was changed, I went to see if Zoey was dressed so that we could go downstairs. Walking into her room, I had to take a moment and watch her and Sasha. They were kissing each other's face, and Sasha thought it was the funniest thing ever.

"Hey, are you two ready to head downstairs?" I asked.

"Yes." She looked up at me, and smiled.

"Before we go down, I would like to give you my gift." I picked Sasha up and led her across the hall and opened the door for her to step inside the room.

"Priest, when did you do this? Oh my God, this is beautiful." She looked at me with tears in her eyes.

"We talked about how you wanted the nursery to look, I hired a designer and gave her your vision." I shrugged. The colors were neutral because we didn't know what we were having, but everything that our child needed was already setup.

"Thank you, I love it." She kissed my cheek and smiled. I grabbed her hand as we walked out to join the family.

"Ahhhh, y'all look so cute," Cas said as we walked outside. Zoey, Sasha, and I wore the same colors. Zoey and I decided not to open gifts until tomorrow. We just wanted to enjoy the day. Cas really did a great job putting all of this together, and Zoey was so happy. I took a seat at the table with the guys and had a few drinks.

"You good, bro?" Nas asked.

"Yeah, I'm good," I replied.

"I have something that I need to talk to you and Pop about. I'm thinking of coming out of the game, I'm having a kid, and I want to be around to watch he or she grow up. The night of Cassie's birthday, I was gone ask her to marry me, but as we all know, that shit went left. I think Cannon would be a good person to take over and run the organization for us," Nas replied.

"Bruh, we would never stop you from coming out. I will always support any decisions you make. I believe you're right Cannon would be a good person for the business." I dapped him up.

"I feel the same way, do what's best for you. I don't want my grandchildren to ever have to be in the streets doing what we've done. I think we've made enough money for them to live good lives, and I'm happy with that," Pop stated, and he's right. None of us ever have to work another day in our life, and our family would be good. Cannon walked up to the table and dapped everyone up.

"Sup with y'all?" He questioned, but his attention was diverted to Tiff when she walked inside the house.

"Y'all might as well hug your cousin, 'cause tonight I'm snatching her ass up, and she won't be out for a while. She gone come back new, changed, and muthafuckin' improved by the time y'all see her ass again." We all burst out laughing because this nigga was crazy.

"Nigga, Tiff don't want your shriveled-up dick. She's

chasing the same shit you're chasing, but I would like to see you try. That shit gone be funny as fuck." Nas ass loved fuckin' with Cannon about Tiff, but we both knew that Cannon was definitely breaking her down.

A couple of hours later, everyone was leaving, and the staff Cas hired had cleaned the grounds.

"Big Mama and Sash are staying at the house for a couple of days," Nas revealed as I sipped my drink.

"That's cool with me, but does Zoey know that Sasha is leaving? She may have a hard time with that one." I shrugged.

"She good with it. Come on, babe. Let's go," Cas said. We dapped it up and they left out. I decided to have a few more drinks, so I sat outside listening to some music, thinking about all the shit that was going on in my life. I had a woman that I loved more than I loved myself, but we just couldn't get this shit right. *You Decide by Usher x Zaytoven* was flowing through the speakers when Zoey walked out onto the patio naked, and all I could do was stare at her.

"Your baby would like a kiss goodnight." She smiled. I sat my drink on the table, grabbing her by her waist, guiding her in between my legs. I began kissing her stomach just as *Climax by Usher* came through the speakers. It was at that moment that I knew I couldn't let her go. She was who I wanted to spend my life with and raise our children together. I continued kissing all over her stomach as my hands roamed her body. I could feel her unraveling in my arms, and that's exactly what I wanted her to do. The love for her was undeniable, and I was done fighting with her.

"Priest!"

"I'm right here, beautiful." I stood pulling her into me, kissing her lips as she slid her tongue inside of my mouth. I lifted her up and carried her inside, lying her on the couch as I removed my clothes.

"Priest! Ohhhhh, I need you!" She cried out, as I ran my tongue across her pussy.

"You got me. I will be right here giving you everything that you need." I sucked her clit into my mouth, as she screamed out in ecstasy.

"Uhhhh, I'm about to cum," she whimpered.

"Mmmm hmmm, that's what I want you to do. Cum, baby," I growled as I sucked the hell out of her clit. She began shaking and screaming my name, and that shit was driving me insane. I turned her on her side and eased into her with force.

"Ohhhh God! I can't take it," she moaned, and I slowed my movements down because she's pregnant. I was deep stroking her, but I swear the way this pussy was set up, I was ready to murder this pussy.

"Damn, this pussy is crazy. I love you, beautiful," I gritted.

"Shhhhiit! I love you too. I don't want you to be with anyone else. I want you to be with me! I need you with me! I'm sorry. Ohhhhh, fuck," she whispered, and hearing her say that shit caused the savage to come out in my ass. And that's what she got tonight, savagely fucked.

"I'm right here, Zoe. You're all that I will ever need," I spoke as I deep stroked her, and I could feel the cum rising out of me.

"Yesss! Oh, fuck yesss! I'm cumming!" She screamed and we both released together.

"Priest?"

"Yeah, baby?" I looked at her.

"I want some ice cream now. I was thinking about it when we were fuckin', but I wanted you more than the ice cream. Now that we're done, can you feed me some ice cream?" I looked at her, and we both just burst into laughter.

"Come on, let's clean up, and I will make sure to feed you all the ice cream your heart desires. Once we were done with our session in the shower, we were in bed, and I was feeding her ice cream.

"This is so good; you really should go get you some." She smiled, and I chuckled.

"Why do I have to go get some, when I can just share with you?" I asked her, and she was shaking her head no.

"Mmmm, mmmm, there is only enough here for me and the baby." She was serious about that shit. She didn't want to share with me.

"Zoey, are you sure that I'm the man that you want to be with? Can you see being with me for the rest of your life?" I asked her.

"I'm sure. I was miserable without you. I was angry and needed to know in my heart that you wouldn't treat me like that again. I'm sorry that I didn't listen to you about Ty. I promise you I've never done anything with him other than a kiss. And that was when you first found out about him. I realized that I didn't want to lead him on because my heart was with you. I truly just wanted to be his friend, and I acted that way because I didn't want you to dictate who I could and couldn't be friends with. Now I know that you were only trying to protect me," she stated, and she was right to a certain degree.

"This is true, but another reason I didn't want you to be with the nigga is because you were my woman, no matter what the hell you were saying. I hoped at some point we would work our issues out and get back to loving each other. Zoey, you are my lifeline. None of this shit doesn't work without you. My daughter loves you with her whole little heart, and I love you." I leaned in, and we shared a passionate kiss. I dipped some ice cream on the spoon and placed it gently in her mouth.

"Ohhhh, they didn't crush this strawberry up, and it's hard." Her face was frowned. She took it out of her mouth, stared at it and then looked up at me.

"Priest, what... Oh my God, what is this?" She asked, and I was praying the entire time that her greedy ass didn't swallow it.

"It's a circle of love, dedication, commitment, and my desire to have you as my wife. This is me letting you know that I don't want to do this thing called life without you. The girl you saw me talking to works for me, and when she came by earlier, she dropped this off. I started designing this ring at your house the night we made love, and you told me you wasn't sure about us getting back together." I wiped the tears from her eyes and pulled her into my arms.

"Yes, I will marry you!" She cried. My heart began beating so damn fast I thought it would burst out of my chest. I slid the ten-karat princess cut diamond on her finger and kissed her lips. After seeing how she responded to me going out the other day, and having the talk with Nas, I knew that I wanted to ask her to marry me.

I'm so happy everything turned out good yesterday for Zoey's baby shower. I was tickled to death at her being mad as hell, thinking that Priest had a new girl. I wanted to tell her so bad that Dana worked for him, but I felt like she needed that boost to go get her man by any means necessary. Nas, Big Mama, and I were sitting in the kitchen talking while she cooked breakfast.

"Y'all think our plan worked?" Nas asked us.

"I hope like hell it did. When she came up in the room steaming hot over Dana, I told her not to let that big booty heifer get my grandson and become Sasha's step mammy," Big Mama laughed.

"Yessss, Big Mama! When she came to me going off, I didn't say one word about knowing who Dana really was. I wanted her to fight for her man. Now let's hope she did that shit, instead of going to damn sleep." I shook my head and we all burst out laughing.

"Eat-eat," Sasha spoke, and I handed her a piece of bacon. My phone sounded of letting me know I had a text message, and Nas picked his phone up as well.

"Ohhhhhhh, shit! It fuckin' worked!" I screamed, jumping out of my seat, high-fiving Nas. We were hype as hell in this kitchen, Sasha was clapping and her lil' ass didn't know what she was clapping for.

"What happened, let me see?" Big Mama questioned, and Nas showed her the picture of that big ass rock on Zoey's finger. I dialed her number quick as hell and placed the call on speaker.

"Cas, I'm getting marriedddd!" She screamed, and that caused us to scream again.

"Congrats, sis! I'm so happy for you and Priest. That ring is sooooo freaking gorgeous. You two deserve all the happiness in the world."

"Congratulations, granddaughter," Big Mama said to Zoey.

"Thank you, Big Mama! When are you and my lil' munchkin coming home?" Zoey asked her.

"Girl, you need to be over there making up for lost time, not worried about us coming home." We all laughed because Big Mama was crazy. I walked off to talk to Zoey in private. She was extremely happy and we both were in tears. This is how things should be for her, happy and in love. When I ended my call with Zoey, I walked back into the kitchen and Nas was on the phone with Priest and Kash. Everyone was excited about their engagement; it was a joyous time for the Chamber Family.

Walking into the bedroom, I was still so hype about my cousin getting married. I wanted to call my mom so badly, but I knew Zoey would want to give her the good news. Nas walked into the room with the biggest smile on his face.

"Yo, I'm happy as hell that they back together. 'Cause if our damn plan didn't work, I was throwing in the towel. Getting people back together is stressful, and ion want to do that shit no more," Nas said, looking over at me, and I couldn't help but laugh at his ass.

"Babe, do you have something planned for today?" I asked him.

"Nah, I'm going to relax around the house with y'all today. I was thinking that we should start picking up some things for the baby and getting the nursery set up. I will leave that up to you, just tell me who I need to pay for doing the job." I love that he's excited about becoming a father. We went back downstairs to hang out with Big Mama and Sasha.

"I just hung up with your daddy, his ass act like he didn't have time to talk to me again. I need you to take me over there to see what the hell is going on," Big Mama fussed.

"He's trying to make sure things are good with Eva. You need to leave that man alone and let him give you a new daughter in-law. I saw you over there laughing with her at the baby shower. I thought maybe you had a change of heart and was gone give her a chance," Nas said to Big Mama.

"I told you I like her. It's just something about her that's not sitting right with me. She be too damn jumpy for me, looking all around like somebody after her ass." Big Mama was shaking her body and looking all around, trying to show us how Eva be acting. I couldn't hold my laughter in. This lady was a whole mess.

"Man, I'm about to watch some television. I can't be foolin' with yo' ass today. Just trust me when I tell you that stepmama is a good person. And I think she's the perfect woman for Pop, you just need to chill and let them do them."

Big Mama sat back in her chair and didn't say anything else about it. I had to agree with Nas, I loved Eva for Kash, and I'm just hoping that they can get this nigga that's bothering her. I felt bad for her when she was telling us what was going on and how the dude destroyed her house. I told her to call me if she ever wanted to talk because I knew exactly how she was feeling. I hope that they found him soon so that she could get some normalcy back into her life.

ONE MONTH LATER

I was lying down, trying to take a nap, and a pain shot through my body. The pain was so unbearable, I tried getting out of bed. As soon as I stood, another pain shot through me again. I sat back down on the bed until the pain subsided, and I was able to get up and walk to the intercom.

"Priest, it's time," I spoke into the intercom just as another pain hit me, and I felt the rush of fluid come out of me. I was supposed to have my baby in New York but decided that I wanted a water birth delivery, so we found a midwife here in Philadelphia.

"Zoey, I'm right here, baby. I need for you to breathe through the pain," he coached, lifting me and placing me back in the bed. He called Sheila, our midwife, and she said that she would be here shortly.

"Ahhhhhhhhh!" I screamed out; the pain was so damn intense. I wanted to have the baby naturally, but I was damn near ready to tell him to take me to the hospital, so I could get some drugs in my system. Priest removed my clothes and put a tank top on me, then he went into his closet to quickly change his clothes.

"Grandson, is she alright?" Big Mama asked, walking into the room.

"She's in labor. Can you call Cas and tell her to get here now?" I told Cas I wanted her to be here when I went into labor. He began massaging and rubbing my body down to make me feel comfortable. It took Sheila about fifteen minutes to get here and she went right into action.

"Zoey, I'm going to check you to see how far you've dilated, and then I will get the delivery pool ready for you," she stated.

"Ok," I cried because I was having another contraction. Priest was so amazing through this process; he had a delivery pool installed for me to give birth in.

"Alright, she's ten centimeters dilated. It's time to have a baby. Priest, I'm going to get the pool started, and you need to get her downstairs. Zoey, remember you have to breathe through the contractions," Sheila said and walked out of the room. A few minutes later, Cas and my aunt Crystal came running into the bedroom.

"It's time to have us a baby!" She clapped in excitement.

"It's time." I smiled.

"Everything is going to be alright, Zoey." My aunt Crystal rubbed my hair and smiled at me.

"Ok, babe, I have to carry you down to the birthing pool." He lifted me into his arms and carried me downstairs. None of the family was allowed to come over until after the baby was born, because of the nature of my delivery. But there was no way that I was having this baby without Cas and Aunt Crystal.

"Urgghhhhhhhhh! I think it's coming out. Ohhhhh My Goddd!" I screamed, and Priest sat me in the water and then got in behind me. He began massaging my shoulders, thighs, and stomach.

"Zoey, I can see your baby's head, and on the next contraction, I want you to push," Sheila instructed, and as soon as the contraction started, I began pushing. As Priest started speaking in my ear.

"Zoey, the moment I saw you, I knew that you were the design that God created just for me. I wanted the very essence of you. I wanted a love so rare and true with you that only God could breakthrough. I breathe you, I need you, I want you, I love you, and I yearn for you. I gave you my heart and allowed you to undress my soul. Mon amour pour toi ne vacilleria jamais, je te donne mon coeur pour toujours (My love for you will never waiver. I give you my heart forever.)" Just as he finished talking, I pushed the baby out and everyone was in tears.

"It's a boy!" she yelled, and I was a complete mess with

tears flowing. My baby was here. I couldn't believe that I had given birth to this beautiful baby boy. Going through so many heartbreaks with miscarriages, I was finally able to look into my baby's face, smell him, and hold him. I looked at Priest and he had the same tears as I did. When the baby opened his eyes, he looked right into the eyes of his father. Priest cut the cord and Sheila took the baby, weighed him, and cleaned him up.

"Damn, I want to have my baby the exact same way. The shit you just did was deep as hell. Ion care if I don't know what the hell you were talking about, Nas ass better talk his shit the French way. Priest, you need to go over and teach yo' brother how to before I deliver, 'Cause babbby, you did that shit! Congrats to you both, he's absolutely beautiful," Cas said as she admired the baby.

"Congratulations to the both of you. He's so handsome. What is his name going to be?" Aunt Crystal asked.

"Priest Amir Chamber, Jr." I smiled, looking over at Priest. We talked about what we would name our baby if it was a girl or boy, and the name fits him perfectly, because he looked just like his father. Once Sheila took care of me, Priest was able to carry me back upstairs, and I got cleaned up. I loved the fact that I didn't have to go to the hospital at all. The baby's pediatrician was here checking him out. If I had it my way, I would have water birth deliveries with all of my children. I do plan on having more children, but I'm definitely waiting a couple of years.

"He is so perfect," I said to Priest.

"Yes, he is. You did good, baby." He kissed my lips.

"He is a perfectly healthy baby. we weighed him at 8lbs & 5oz and he's 22 inches long," Dr. Morris stated.

"Ok, thank you." Priest shook his hand and I smiled.

"I would like to see him in my office next week. I will have my office call you with a day and time. Congratulations to you both," Dr. Morris stated and left out. Nas, Big Mama, Kash, and Eva came into the room, and everyone was full of joy to meet the newest addition to the family.

"Somebody is here to meet her brother," Cas said as Sasha ran into the room.

"Mommie, it's a baby!" She clapped, and we all laughed at her.

"This is your baby brother, Sash." I kissed her on the cheek, and she kissed her brother on his head. Sheila came in and said she would be over to check on us tomorrow then she left. The family visited with us for about an hour, and they all left so that the baby and I could get some rest. Priest never left our side, and Sasha stayed in the room with us until she fell asleep.

Being a mother was the best thing I have ever experienced. I was getting back to my old self. The baby weight was easing off of me, but I had some work to do. Priest Sasha, PJ, and I were going out for lunch since I had been stuck inside for a little over six weeks, only going out for appointments. I decided that I would stay here indefinitely, and when I needed to go back to New York for work, my family would go with me. I called Blu and told them that they could cancel the lease on my brownstone. We were going up in a couple of weeks to move my things out of the house.

"Are you ready, babe?" He asked.

"Yep, I can't wait to get me a steak from Del Frisco's." We were all dressed in jeans, white shirts, and some white Nikes. The baby's jeans were a little too big for him, but we made it work. About thirty minutes later, we were pulling into the Media courthouse.

"Babe, why are we at the courthouse?" I asked, looking over at him.

"Zoey, the other night you said to me that we should just go to the courthouse and get married. That you didn't want to have a big wedding, did you mean it?" He asked me, and the tears were building up.

"Yes, I meant it. Is that why we're here? Oh, my God! Are we about to get marrriiiedd?! Hell yeah, let's go get married!" I screamed out my excitement, and he laughed at me.

"I promise you we don't have to do this. I will give you whatever type of wedding you want. You just say the word, and it's yours, but I need to be married to you as soon as possible," he said and I kissed the hell out of this man.

"Mmmm, mmm, this is the one I want right here. But wait, I can't get married without Cas, and my Aunt Crystal. They will kill me!" I looked over at him.

"I kind of wanted this to be just us," he explained, and I

agreed. I would do anything for him. I knew they would be upset about not being here, but as long as I had my kids here, I was ok. It was true I didn't want a big wedding, and I would marry this man butt ass naked if I had to.

Priest and I filed for our marriage license, but they said the judge couldn't do the ceremony today. I was disappointed because he had this all planned out for us. I didn't even want to go out to eat anymore, so Priest said he would cook dinner when we got back home.

"Babe, don't be upset. You're going to be my wife soon enough." He smiled.

"Well, I would have liked for it to be today," I said and he laughed at my antics.

"It's not funny, why did the lil' stupid judge have to get sick? And it's a courthouse, they should be full of damn judges," I fussed all the way home and was still fussing as we walked inside the house. I could have sworn I saw a white lady with a bouquet of flowers walk pass out on the patio.

"Priest, I just saw someone walk pass on our patio," I whispered.

"What? There is no one back there," he stated, and I grabbed my baby out of the carrier and Sasha's hand while he went to go check it out. I was about to haul ass upstairs and put my kids in the saferoom and do a Big Mama on their ass.

"Babe, come look. There is no one out here," he said.

"I know what the hell I saw," I told him, walking up to the patio door, peeking out, and I almost dropped my damn baby. There were beautiful white and yellow roses everywhere and our backyard was decorated beautifully. Our family was here clapping and cheering us on, and I was in total shock.

"Girl, bring yo' ass on out this door. It's hot as hell and I need me a drink!" Nas shouted.

"Priest, are we really doing this?" I asked him as the tears streamed down my face.

"Yes, I said I wanted to marry you today, not tomorrow. I just wanted to make it a special moment, but we still getting married in these jeans. Nah, I'm joking. They're waiting for you upstairs." He smiled, as Cas and Tiff came inside to take me upstairs. It took me about an hour to get dressed. I wore a simple white Vera Wang dress, and Cas did my makeup.

Once we were done, we went downstairs, and the ceremony started. *Giving Myself by Jennifer Hudson* began playing, and I walked down the aisle. Priest was standing with our son in his arms, and Sasha was standing next to him. They had changed their clothes as well, and I couldn't control the tears. I couldn't believe that I was marrying this handsome man right now; my heart was so full at this moment. The wedding started, and we said our vows.

About twenty-five minutes later, I was Mrs. Priest Amir Chamber. This was so perfect, and I couldn't believe that I married the love of my life. It was a long road for us, and I didn't think we would make it to this point, but it was all worth it. Everyone came up hugging and congratulating us. I was so excited that my Aunt Crystal was here to see me give birth and get married. Later that night, *On Top by Trey Songz* was flowing through the speakers as my husband's tongue graced every part of my body. I was on fire as he worked his way down to my folds.

"I need you, baby." I whimpered as his tongue grazed my clit.

"I'm going to give you everything you need, I promise you that," He spoke licking and sucking on my pussy like he's never done before.

"Mmmmmmm, shit! Please don't stop, fuccckkk," I cried out wrapping my hand around his head pulling him deeper into my pussy, gyrating against his face. This tingling sensation came over my body and I couldn't form words, for what this man was doing to me. Tears streamed down my face as I cried out in ecstasy. He stood up and his dick was so hard and beautiful, I had to touch it. I began stroking him, sliding my tongue up and down his shaft. He bit down on his bottom lip as I sucked him into my mouth applying pressure while moving up and down his dick over and over again.

"Fuck!" He spat. I felt his dick throbbing inside my mouth, and I knew he was about to cum. He tried to pull his dick out, but I wanted to taste him, and he couldn't hold it any longer.

"Fuckkkkkkk, Zoe!" He roared as he released, and I sucked his ass dry. I laid on the bed and he hovered over me sliding his dick up and down my slit easing into me.

"Yessss, baby," I moaned as he slammed inside of me, stroking deeper and deeper into my walls.

"Damn this is pussy is fuckin' amazing!" He growled

pounding on my spot, and I couldn't control myself as my juices began to flow.

"Oh, Goddd!" I screamed.

"Fuckkk!" He growled as he released inside of me. For the rest of the night I made love to my husband.

ONE MONTH LATER

Cas was almost four and a half months pregnant. I loved to see her with her round belly, but that lil' nigga was blocking how I hit the pussy. We found out last week that we were having a boy and we both were excited. Tonight, I was having a party at the club for Cas, and it was a surprise. I wanted to make up for her birthday party that she missed, but she thought that we were just hanging out with Priest and Zoey. My dad and Eva were going to swing by and pick up Ma Crystal for me. I'm glad that she decided to stay until after Cas has the baby. I walked downstairs, and Cas was talking to her mom about the baby's nursery. They were coming out tomorrow to get started on that for us. Cas said she didn't want a baby shower because we had already gotten everything the baby needed. By the time we made it to the club, all the family had made it. I had to make some stops to give my Pop time to get there. *Shake the Room by Pop Smoke ft Quavo* was blasting through the speakers. When we made it up to the VIP section, the DJ gave Cas a shout out, and she looked at me.

"Babe, what the hell is going on?" She asked over the music.

"We're celebrating you tonight. Your birthday was fucked up, and I wanted to recreate the night for you. I had to let everything calm down first," I told her.

When she saw the family, she ran up to everybody giving them hugs. I was glad to see stepmama. Pop said he can barely get her to go out anywhere without him being there. We still haven't been able to find this nigga that was fuckin' with her, but the good thing is that nothing fucked up has happened, and she hasn't been getting any more phone calls. When we do find his ass, you can best believe he gone die.

"What's up, cousin?" Tiff asked, walking up to me with Brittany following behind her.

"Brit, where the hell you been? It's like yo' ass fell off the face of the earth?" I asked her. Brittany and Tiff been friends since the sandbox days.

"I moved out to Cali and just came home to visit. How have you been?" She asked.

"Cooling, 'bout to have a baby," I told her.

"That's great, I just met Priest's wife, and he told me he just had a son. Things have surely changed since I've been gone." She smiled. I forgot her ass had a thing for Priest. If she knew like I knew she would stay away. Zoey plays no games about her husband. Let's just say Dana no longer works for my brother.

"Tiff, yo' nigga said he will be here in a few minutes," I laughed.

"He's not my nigga! I wish dude would leave me the fuck alone. I'm seriously not trying to hook up with his ass," she went off.

"Damn, a dude trying to smash, Tiff? Things have really changed since I've been gone," Brittany said, shaking her head laughing. I walked off laughing, grabbing the mic from the DJ.

"Yooooooo, I want to thank everybody for coming out tonight to celebrate with my baby. She wasn't able to celebrate her birthday the way we wanted to this year, so here we are now. Cas, come here, baby." She walked up to me with her hand over her face.

"Don't embarrass me," she said, and I laughed.

"Well, if you call this embarrassing you, then I guess I'm gone embarrass yo' ass tonight. You know, Bear, I'm not a big romantic nigga, but I tell you and show you that I love you all the time. I want to be in this thing with you for a lifetime, baby. Will you marry me?" I asked her as I got down on one knee, and she was screaming, jumping, and crying tears of joy.

"Girl, you gone say yes, or keep damn screaming?" I asked

her. My damn knee was starting to hurt down here on this hard ass floor.

"Yesss, yesss, baby!" I slid the ring on her finger, and I was glad that I could finally place it there. The night of her birthday that was the big surprise, I was going to ask her to marry me. I had Priest make the ring for me, so he knew that I was going to ask her. We even talked about doing something together, but I believed that every woman's special day should be about them. Her ring was tight as fuck. My brother did a good damn job. It was a 6kt Marquise cut diamond, and it looks fya as fuck on her finger. I pulled her in for a hug and tongued her ass down in this club. My Bear was getting ready to be a married woman.

"Baby, we not doing no weddings, no surprises, none of that shit. We just going to the courthouse and do it. I'm pregnant and about to have our baby, and I just want to do it." She was serious. I was with whatever she wanted, but I knew my girl, she just might change her mind. I felt the same way; I just want to get married and get ready for our baby to come.

"Congrats, you two! OMG! Let me see your ring!" Zoey yelled as they all walked up to me and Cas. Ma Crystal was in tears, and I pulled her in for a hug.

"You did good. Thank you for loving her the way you do," She cried.

"I will always love and protect her," I told her.

"Congrats, son." Pop dapped me up.

"Thank you, Pop. Now it's time for you to make an honest

woman out of Eva. We see the love you have for her. If you ever feel like you want to do it, you can go ahead and do it as far as I'm concerned." I hugged him.

We partied for the rest of the night and it felt good to see my girl smile. I was finally about to lock my Bear down.

Chapter Twenty-Five

KASH

We have been looking all over for this nigga. I haven't been able to locate him, and that shit was eating me the fuck up. All the damn resources we have and nobody can get a location. He hasn't been to his mom's crib because I have had somebody sitting on her shit for the last couple of months. We were having the family over for dinner because I had a surprise for Eva. Everything between us was good, and I loved the hell out of her. She was happy that everyone was coming over. We even borrowed Ms. Carol, and she was coming over to help Eva get everything cooked for tonight. Which she should be here soon because it was already a little after three in the afternoon. Walking into the kitchen, Eva was setting things up for Carol, and I was going to get out of their way. I had to go by the restaurant and pick up the drop from last night.

"You're getting ready to leave, babe?" She asked, walking up to me, kissing my lips.

"Yeah, I should be back by six. Everyone isn't coming over until seven."

"I'm excited to have the family over. We're always at Priest's home, or Nas' and it feels good to have everyone come over to our house all at once." She smiled, and I was smiling at her. That was the first time she said our home. I'm glad she's starting to feel comfortable enough to know that this is indeed her home. I heard the doorbell going off, and I knew that it was Ms. Carol.

"Hey, Kash. It's good to see you. Boy, this is a beautiful home you have," she spoke as she followed me into the kitchen.

"Thank you. I'm happy you finally decided to come visit me and cook in my kitchen," I laughed as I kissed her cheek. Carol was like family to us, and we loved her, just as she loved all of us.

"You know your son takes up all my time. I'm so happy he and Zoey got married. He's so much happier, and I'm glad to see him that way. Eva, what you got over here?" She asked Eva.

"I was thinking we could have a choice of Salmon and Steak tonight," Eva said to her.

"That sounds good, I like to make a sauce to go on my Salmon, and I may need you to run to the store and pick up a few things for me," Ms. Carol told her.

"Ok, let's write out a list, and I will go run and get it." I kissed Eva and told her I would be back in time for dinner. Walking into the restaurant, I spoke to Lonnie and went back to my office to go over some of the paperwork. My phone was going off and it was Nas calling.

"Hey, son."

"What's up, Pop? I was just checking in. Are we still on for Seven?" He asked.

"Yeah, it starts at seven. Don't be late, son. We know how your ass can get. Eva is really excited about everybody coming over," I told him because we could tell Nasir seven, and his ass will come walking in at nine.

"Man, I will be on time, damn! Did you pick the ring up?" He asked.

"Yes, I have it."

"Ohhhhh, shit. stepmama 'bout to be a Chamber! Did you talk to Big Mama about all of this?" He asked.

"Nah, I haven't had the time, but I will talk to her before I ask Eva," I responded.

"Nigga, you better, 'cause this damn shit ain't gone go the way you plan if Claudia Chamber ain't feeling it. And I swear I'mma act like I didn't know shit 'bout none of this." Nas was so fuckin' extra.

"Bye, son!" I hung up on his ass and laughed. I had been working for a couple of hours. Looking at my watch, it was damn near six. I needed to get home and change before everyone got there. Just as I was getting into my car and pulled into traffic, my phone was going off, and I saw that it was Eva.

"Hey, babe. I'm on my way home now."

"Kash, somethings wrong. I don't see Donte and I.... Oh, my God! Noooo!" The call dropped, and so did my fuckin' heart.

"Evaaaa!" I tried calling her back and I got her voicemail. I dialed Nas so that he could meet me at the house.

"Yo," He answered.

"Something is going on at my house! I need for you to meet me there now!" I yelled, ending the call. By the time I pulled up into my driveway, Nas was pulling in behind me, and Priest had pulled up as well. Pulling my gun out, the door to the house was cracked, and I moved inside with the boys behind me.

"Don't move, nigga!" This nigga done walked his bitch ass up in my shit and was holding my woman at gunpoint.

"Kash, you have to do something. Carol is hurt! He said he had to prove a point to me that he wasn't playing and shot her!" Eva cried out.

"Bitch, shut your ass up!" He roared as he pressed the gun into her side.

"Shot who? I know damn well this lil' half-pint mutha-fucka ain't touch Ms. Carol!" Nas roared as he tried to walk into the kitchen.

"If you take another step, I'm going to shoot this bitch. Now all I want is my woman and y'all gone let us out of here. Or her ass is gone die, and nobody will have her!" He shouted.

"Nigga, if you killed Ms. Carol, yo' mama gone die!" Nas told him.

"Eva calm down and close your eyes, baby," I said to her. She stared at me for a moment and then closed her eyes. My gun was already up, and my eyes were trained on this pussy ass nigga. I moved and he flinched pressing his gun into my woman's side, and I could feel the fire inside of me rise. I didn't have shit to say, I let my gun do all the talking lighting his ass up.

"Ahhhhhh, nahh! Not Ms. Carol! What the fuck!" He cried as he kneeled down beside her.

"Fuckkkkkkk!" Priest yelled out as the tears filled his eyes and began to fall.

"Oh my God, I'm so sorry!" Eva cried, and this whole scene was a fuckin' mess. My sons were devastated, and Eva was traumatized.

"Who gone cook me steak, shrimp, and bacon cheeseburgers now?! You stupid muthafucka!" Nas jumped up, walking into the room, kicking and punching the shit out of that nigga.

"Nasir," I called out to calm him.

"What the fuck did Ms. Carol ever do to your lil half-pint looking ass!" He yelled at the dead nigga. I had to pull him away and he sat on the couch in tears.

"I have to call the police, and her husband," Priest said and walked outside. I took Eva upstairs and told her to lay down until the police arrived. This was heartbreaking to see this happen to someone as nice as Carol.

Chapter Twenty-Six

ZOEY

I can't imagine my life without my husband. Everything we have been through was so worth it for me, with the exception of the gun to my head. We had a very long conversation about trust, commitment, understanding, and respecting each other. We wake up each morning and pray together for our marriage and our family. There is no greater love than what I'm experiencing with this man. My heart breaks for him right now because he's devastated by the death of Ms. Carol. She was loved by this family, and we're going to miss her. For the last few days, we've gone downstairs and expected her to be in the kitchen. Our son is healthy and growing, and Sasha loves her little brother. My heart is full when I look at my children, and I love every moment of being a mother to them. I went into the nursery to check on Priest Jr., and his father was rocking him back to sleep.

"I didn't hear him crying through the monitor," I said to him as I sat in the chair beside him.

"I took the monitor out of the room so that you can get some rest." He smiled, and my heart melted.

"Thank you. I know that you're not feeling your best, are you going to work today?" I asked him.

"Nah, I have some things to do today. Why don't you get dressed and come hang out with your husband for a little while? Big Mama will watch the kids for us," he requested.

"Ok, that sounds like a good idea. I should be ready in about thirty minutes." I kissed him and PJ and walked out of the room to get dressed. It took me about forty minutes to get myself together. Walking downstairs, I heard Priest in the kitchen talking to his grandmother.

"Hey, baby. You slept good today because you missed breakfast, and it's almost time for lunch," she said as I kissed her cheek.

"I needed that rest, and I'm sure my handsome husband will buy his wife some lunch while we're out." I smiled.

"Beautiful lady, I would buy you a restaurant if you wanted it." He winked at me.

"Y'all go ahead on and enjoy your day; I got these babies. Priest, are y'all taking the food over to Carol's family tonight?" She asked.

"Yeah, I spoke to her husband, and he couldn't believe that we were feeding the family tonight and for the repast. I want to do more, and I will do more for him. I just have to figure it all out at this point. I'm still so pissed and hurt that she's gone. If that nigga wasn't already dead, I would kill him with my bare hands. He didn't just take a cook from us; she was our family, and she had a family of her own that loved her."

I felt so bad about this whole thing. The guys were taking this really bad. I called Cas last night, and she said that Nas wasn't doing good at all. Priest and I left out, and he stopped by the shop first to pick up a few things. I wasn't fuckin' with the Dana bitch at all. I walked in to bring my husband lunch one day, and this hoe walked into his office and sat down on the desk with her damn legs gapped open. While I was sitting there! Nahhhh, we not gone do none of that shit. I would never tell my husband how to run his business and who he can hire, but that day I fired that bitch myself, and he was perfectly fine with it. He said if I hadn't done it, he would have because she was disrespectful as fuck for doing that shit. We were pulling into the courthouse, and I knew it wasn't about us, so he must have some business to handle here.

"Come inside with me, this won't be long," he spoke, and I got out of the car. When we got inside, his attorney was inside, and I was a little confused as to what was going on.

"Priest, Zoey, it's good to see you both. We have everything together, and all you both have to do is sign, and you're good to go," he stated.

"What are we signing?" I questioned as Priest pulled me over to the side.

"Zoey, the night our whole world was turned upside down taught me so many lessons. I was at fault for a lot of things, but there was one thing that I should have been sure of, and that's how much you love Sasha. I will forever be sorry for the mistake I made and how I treated you. Even through all of that, my love for you was real. It just took God a moment to get me together. Today, I would like to make our family whole by asking you to adopt Sasha. We already know that she's your daughter. I don't think she would have it any other way, but I would love it if we can make this official. Can you be the mother of both of my children?" He asked me. I was so full of tears and happiness that my heart felt as if it was going to explode.

"You want me to adopt, Sasha? Like she's going to be my baby girl for real?" I looked at him because I had to be clear that this is really happening.

"Yes." He smiled as he wiped the tears from my eyes. I ran back to the attorney and left Priest behind.

"Where do I sign?" I asked, and he pointed to where my signature was supposed to go. Once Priest signed the document, the judge signed off on it, and we left the courthouse. I was so emotional that I couldn't stop crying, and all I wanted to do was to kiss and love on my daughter.

"Priest, can you please take me home?" I told him, and he grabbed my hand.

"Babe, are you okay?" He asked.

"Yes, please just take me home." When he pulled into the driveway, I jumped out of the car, leaving my purse and husband behind and took off running into the house. Sasha was in the family room playing with her brother, and I picked her up, holding her tight.

"Sasha, mommy loves you so much. I promise to never leave your side, baby girl." I cried. This completed me. Priest will never understand what he did for me today. I have loved this little girl from the moment I saw her. She may not be my biological daughter, but I love her just as much as I love her brother. She's my forever baby girl.

Chapter Twenty-Seven

CASSIE

Nas really got me when he asked me to marry him. My emotions are still all over the place. I can't believe how much we both have grown together, and the love that I have for this man is crazy. I could remember all the times I tried to push him away when he was trying to get at me. I'm so glad that he never gave up because I would have never known what it would feel like to be in love with a man like this. It was a little after one in the afternoon, and I went downstairs to check on Nas. He was in a bad mood, and I wanted to do something to get him out of this funk.

"Babe, how are you feeling? Do you need anything?"

"No, if you can't bring Ms. Carol back then, I don't need nothing. I think we need to go find out where they buried that punk-ass, lil small fry ass nigga and set his grave on fire.

He should burn in hell for what he did. I swear me and Tiff ready to find his family and beat the shit out of them niggas. The only way them niggas getting a pass if they under the age of sixteen, everybody else is getting this work!" He yelled.

"Babe, you can't just go around beating up people that didn't have anything to do with the fucked-up shit he did," I said. And what the fuck I say that shit for.

"Yes, the fuck we can! Ms. Carol ain't have shit to do with his Stuart Little fuckin' ass shit he had going on, but he involved her. All she was trying to do was cook us dinner; she didn't go there to cook steak, salmon, and a side of bullets. On some real shit, Cas, I'm fuckin' a few people up behind this shit," he blurted.

"I'm sorry you're hurting, babe. Is there anything I can do to make you feel better?" I asked as I sat on his lap, kissing his lips.

"You can give me some bereavement pussy, and I think that will make me feel a lil' better." I almost laughed, but I didn't want to make fun of him at a time like this. My baby was in mourning, and he needed me to make him feel better.

"I love you, babe." I kissed his lips again. He stood with me in his arms and carried me upstairs. He pulled my tank top off and began gliding his tongue across my breast. I threw my head back as he latched on, sucking the hell out of my nipple.

"Mmmmm, shit!" I blurted, as he began kissing all over my body. Grazing his fingers across my clit caused me to jump. My pussy was on fire. Every time this man touched me, I get this sensation that runs through my body.

"Damn, this pussy wet as fuck, Bear," he whispered.

"Fuck," I gritted out, trying to hold it together, but I was losing it. He was working the hell out of my pussy with his fingers. He laid on the bed, and I hovered over him, easing down on his dick, causing us both to moan out in pleasure.

"This pussy is so fuckin' good, god damn!" He growled as he grabbed my waist, guiding me up and down on his dick.

"Ohhhh shit! Right there, babe! That's my fuckin' spot!" I moaned as he deep stroked my insides. He pulled out of me so he could hit it from behind, and my pussy was soaking wet. He slammed inside of me repeatedly, and I was screaming for dear life. I knew my mom heard us because we just didn't give a fuck.

"Yessss! Oh God! Fuck the shit out of me!" I screamed, and he did just that. I was squirting every damn where it was as if I was having an outer body experience. I couldn't stop cumming as he thrust deep inside of me.

"Urggggghhh, shit!" He roared as he released inside of me so damn hard I could feel it hitting my walls. We lay there for a few minutes, and I climbed out of bed to go clean up. I have got to stop fuckin' with his ass. I think we both be forgetting that I'm pregnant. Zoey was right; I have been wanting to fuck more and more since I've been pregnant and Nas ass doesn't mind one bit.

After my shower, I walked into my walk-in closet to find something to wear for the day. I heard my phone ringing, and I knew it was Zoey. We were supposed to go check on Eva. She wasn't doing too good, and we wanted to let her know that we're here if she needs us. I ran out of the closet to grab my phone.

"Hey, are you on your way?" I asked her.

"I'm outside, heifer. I sent you a text letting you know I was on my way," she said.

"Ok, give me a few minutes, and I will be right out." I hung up and pulled a maxi dress out to wear, matching it up with a pair of Gucci slides. After I lotioned my body down, I got dressed and grabbed my things.

"Babe, Zoe is outside. I will be back in a few hours." I kissed his lips.

"Alright, I will see you later. Be careful and take your time going down the stairs, Bear," he yelled out. When I got downstairs, my mom was in the family room relaxing. She was loving it here and we loved having her. While she was gone, Nas called a contractor to start the plans of building a two-bedroom guest house out back. I'm so happy that we have enough room on our property to do it.

"Mom, I will be back later. Zoe and I are going to check on Eva," I said to her, and she got up to walk me out the door.

"Ok, I'm gone get dinner started soon. Hey, baby!" My mom yelled out to Zoe.

"Hey, auntie. I love you!" Zoey spoke to her as I got into the car, and she pulled off.

"Girl, you are glowing. What yo' husband over there doing to yo' ass?" I asked her.

"Loving me the way a man should. I have been on a cloud so high, Cas. I can't even explain how that man makes me feel, and when he asked me to adopt Sasha, that just elevated my love for him. The relationship I had with Dom doesn't even compare to what I have now. He caters to my heart, and I've never had that before."

"Well damn. Girl, let me say this. When that nigga started speaking to you in English and French, I was ready to sign my man up to the school of Priest, so his ass could take French 101. I love me a fluent nigga." I looked at her, and we both burst out laughing.

"You need help. I hope we can cheer Eva up. I spoke with Pop this morning, and he said that she has been in tears every day. I think she believes that we might blame her for what happened to Ms. Carol," Zoey stated.

"I hope she doesn't feel that way because that shit is not her fault. She didn't know what that crazy nigga was up to. He killed Kash's guard, and the police found his body on the side of the house." We pulled into Kash's driveway and got out of the car. Zoe rang the doorbell, and we waited for someone to open the door.

"Hey, ladies. Come on in; she's upstairs." Kash opened the door. We hugged him and went upstairs.

"Eva, how are you feeling?" Zoe asked her.

"Hey, ladies. I'm trying to pull myself together. I just can't believe that I got myself in a situation like that. I never thought he was that type of person. When I told him that I couldn't see him anymore, I didn't think he would go crazy like this. I feel so horrible, and I keep seeing Carol's face when he lifted the gun on her. I will never forgive myself for what happened to her!" She cried.

"Eva, you can't blame yourself for what happened. You didn't know this would happen." I sat down beside her and wrapped my arms around her.

"I really appreciate you girls coming over. It means a lot." She wiped her eyes. For the next few hours, we sat around and talked with Eva and Kash. I believe with time she will be alright. I love the way Kash loves her and I'm happy that he's found love again. I pray that this family as a whole can find peace and happiness. I can't wait to meet my son, and I damn sure can't wait for Nas to become my husband. I'm in a happy space, and I'm so grateful that God has blessed me with love and an abundance of happiness.

Chapter Twenty-Eight

PRIEST

I was feeling down because today was Ms. Carol's funeral. I loved that lady like a mother. We had a great relationship, and she loved my family. Nas and I went over and spent time with her family last night, and we heard so many great stories about her.

"I'm ready," my wife spoke as she entered the family room.

"Big Mama, we will be back as soon as we can." Zoey and I kissed our kids, and we walked out of the house.

"We have to stop by and pick up Nas and Cas," I said to Zoe, as I held her hand.

"Ok, did Lonnie get all the food over to the church?" She asked.

"Yeah, he called me a couple of hours ago. He said that everything was set, and the staff was there to serve the food. Pop was serious about closing Bianca's down for the day." Pop and Eva felt bad that Ms. Carol died because of the issues Eva was having. Pop paid for Ms. Carol's and his guard Donte's funeral expenses.

At first, we assumed dude had help, but he didn't. When we looked at the camera recordings, we saw him walk up on Donte, and he shoot him. This nigga really had this shit planned out, but he wasn't expecting Ms. Carol to be inside the house. It was heartbreaking to see it all go down on recording. Thank God Pop wasn't charged for killing his punk ass. Pulling into Nas' driveway, he and Cas came out a few minutes later.

"That was nice of Kash," Zoey replied. Nas and Cas got into the car and I backed out. By the time we made it to the church, it was packed and cars were everywhere.

"I hope we can find a seat because my pregnant ass don't feel like standing all that time," Cas fussed, and I'm sure we would be able to at least get her and Zoe a seat.

"Let's go, so we can make sure to get a seat for y'all," Nas said, and we got out of the car, heading into the church. We saw Pop and Eva seated, and thank God they saved us a seat.

About ten minutes later, the family was coming inside, and the services started. When the woman got up and sung, *Take Me to The King by Tamela Mann,* I could no longer hold my tears. It was a very emotional funeral. Nas had to get up and walk out I knew he was going to take it hard. He played all day with Ms. Carol and acted up about her cooking, but he really loved her. He's the one that came to me and asked if I wanted to go in with him to buy her a car for her birthday.

This nigga wanted to buy her a hot pink corvette, thank God I was there with him. I could laugh now, but I couldn't imagine Ms. Carol in a hot pink corvette. I will never forget the day we gave her the car, and what that meant for Nas and I. After the service and burial, we went back to the church for the repast.

"Priest, thank you for everything you and your family have done. Carol loved you and your family, and I know how much you all meant to her." Chester held out his hand and I shook it.

"Thank you. I can't tell you how much she meant to me. Ms. Carol and I had a lot of talks. She shared things with me about her wanting you to retire, and at some point, her retiring and y'all moving to Florida. She said that you loved Florida, and I wanted to do something for you to make life a little easier. She loved you, and she absolutely adored her grandchildren. My wife and I will be paying for your grand children's college tuition. I also purchased you a home in Boca Raton, Fl you can move into it whenever you're ready. In this envelope is all the information that you would need regarding the house, and there is a check inside for you. I will always keep in touch with you and make sure you're alright. None of this will ever compare to your wife, but I want to make sure that I honor her the right way. I'm only giving you what I would have given to her when she finally decided to retire." I handed him the envelope, and he and his daughter cried.

"I don't know what to say, but thank you," he stated.

"You don't have to thank me; we wanted to do this for

you. I will check on you in a few days," I told him, and he shook my hand and hugged Zoey. Nas, Cas, Pop, and Eva all spoke, gave him their respects, and we all left.

"Man, that was a sad service, and all I want to do is go home, drink and eat bacon cheeseburgers in honor of Ms. Carol." I looked at my crazy ass brother and shook my head. Once Zoe and I dropped them off, we went home and relaxed for the rest of the day.

"I love you." Zoey walked up to me as I sat out on our bedroom deck.

"I love you too, pretty lady. Is the baby sleep? I asked her.

"Yes, I fed him, and he was out. I just gave Sasha a bath and now she's watching television. She's so excited that her birthday is coming and can't wait for her birthday party," she laughed.

"Yeah, I know. She told me that she wanted a princess dress for her and her mommy." I smiled, as my phone lit up and I saw that it was Chester calling me. I would call him back in the morning. I'm sure he was calling about the five hundred-thousand-dollar check that was inside the envelope.

"That's my baby, always thinking of her mommy. Cas sent me over the contract for the new clothing line company. I will have to go to Los Angeles for two weeks, are you coming with me and the kids? Cause I'm not leaving my babies behind, sir." I burst out laughing at this woman. She never wants to leave her kids.

"Yes, I'm not letting my family go away for two weeks, and I'm not there with you," I told her as I pulled her into my lap.

"I think it's time for you to give me another baby," I said to her.

"I can't do it. Nope, maybe you can get another one out of me in a couple of years." She shrugged.

"Girl, you crazy as hell. You're about to open those fuckin' legs, and we gone reproduce in a couple of minutes." She burst out laughing, and I lifted her into my arms, carrying her inside. I made love to my wife for the rest of the night. This is how love should be. I never want to spend my time arguing with my wife when I could be loving her. Zoey was a beautiful woman, and I thank God for creating her just for me.

Chapter Twenty-Nine

NAS

FOUR MONTHS LATER

Cas and I were in King of Prussia Mall picking up the last of the things that we needed for the baby's arrival.

"I think we have everything we need now, babe. If you think of anything else, I can just come back and pick it up. We've been in this damn mall for four hours, and I have made three trips to the car," I fussed. My ass was ready to get the hell out of this mall.

"You're right, I'm hungry and tired anyway. Ohhhh shit!" Cas yelled and I turned to look at her.

"What's wrong? Why the hell you standing like that? Cas, I know damn well yo' ass ain't pee on these people floor. I swear I'm about to leave your embarrassing ass right here.

These people about to talk about your ass all by your damn self." I couldn't believe she did that shit.

"Nasir! I think my water just broke!" She screamed.

"What, you bout to have our baby in the damn mall? Come on, we got to get you out of here." I took off running and stopped because I forgot my girl.

"Sir, is everything alright?" The security guard asked me.

"She's in labor." I picked Cas up and carried her out as she screamed out in pain.

"Nas, I don't know if we're going to make it! This baby feels like it's coming," she said as I put her in the back seat and buckled her in.

"Close your legs tight, and keep that lil' nigga in, Cas. He can't come out in my damn car. His ass gotta wait until we get to the hospital." I was nervous as hell. I flew out of the parking lot and headed to the hospital.

"Nasir, this shit hurts! You need to drive this fuckin' car!" Cas yelled. It was a Saturday, and the traffic was crazy trying to get out of King of Prussia. It took about twenty minutes to get to the hospital, and by the time I pulled into the emergency department, my girl was screaming for dear life. I jumped out of the car, ran into the hospital to get some help, and they came rushing out to get Cas out of the car.

"The baby is comingggg!" Cas cried, and we tried to lift her up, but the baby's head was out.

"Wait, don't touch her! We need a doctor and a gurney." One of the nurses told another nurse, and she took off running. A few minutes later, it seemed like half of the hospital staff was outside.

"Sir, I need to check her, what's her name?" He asked.

"Her name is Cassie," I answered.

"Cassie, I'm Dr. Caleb. I need to check you to see how the baby is doing," he said, and Cas just nodded because she was in so much pain. Once he was done and had the baby's head secured, they eased her out of the car and onto the gurney.

"Ohhhhh, God! I need to pussshhhhhh! My baby is coming out now! Urggghhhhhhhhh!" She screamed. I was so damn nervous I was ready to smoke ten damn blunts to the head, and I don't damn smoke.

"The baby is out! We have to go!" Dr. Caleb yelled and they took off. I ran to the security guard and asked him to move my car. I can't believe my girl had half of the damn baby in the car and the other half of his ass outside! I ran behind them, and we all got on the elevator with my girl and son crying.

"I love you, Bear. Everything is going to be alright." I grabbed her hand. Once we got off the elevator, they rushed her into a delivery room.

"Sir, would you like to cut the cord?" He asked, and I walked over and cut my lil' man's cord. They placed the baby on Cas' chest, and she kissed his forehead with a face full of tears. Now I wasn't doing that shit, they gone have to clean his lil' ass up before I put my lips on him.

"He's so perfect, Nasir," she said, looking at me. My heart was about to burst. My guy was a perfect mix of me and his mother. Cas was still in pain, and they had to make sure they got the afterbirth out of her. The nurse took the baby to weigh him, and we never took our eyes off of him.

"Damn, babe, our fuckin' son is here. This shit is wild. I will call the family as soon as we can get things calmed down."

"He's 7lbs & 6oz, and 21 inches," the nurse revealed as she handed the baby to Cas, and we were both amazed at our lil' guy.

"Babe, look at him. I can't believe we made such a beautiful baby." She smiled up at me.

"Girl, he handsome, with his lil' dramatic ass. How half of yo' ass is born in a car and the other half outside? I still can't get over that shit. I'm just grateful that you two are alright. I guess we need to call the family and let them know he's here. I will get Priest to bring your mom up here. About an hour later, Priest, Zoey, and Ma Crystal walked into the room.

"Ahhhhhh, congrats you two! Look at him," Zoey said as she took him out of my arms.

"Hey, grandson. You're so adorable. I hate I missed his birth," Ma Crystal spoke.

"Ma, we almost missed it," I laughed and told them what happened. Pop and Eva came walking into the room.

"Look at this guy, congrats y'all," Pops said, and he was just as excited as we were to meet his grandson.

"What is his name?" Eva asked.

"Omari Nasir Chamber, his dad wanted him to have his

own name. He said he didn't want to share his whole name with my baby." Cas rolled her eyes, and I laughed.

"I said I wanted my young King to have his own identity. He still has a part of my name and I'm cool with that," I told them. This was everything I needed. I never thought that I would have my own little family. The love I have for them is an amazing feeling, and I wouldn't want it any other way. Now all I have to do is to marry this beautiful woman.

Chapter Thirty

KASH

ONE YEAR LATER

The entire family is on vacation in St. Lucia, and it was much needed for all of us. Everything was back to normal, and Eva was getting back to being the beautiful, strong woman that she was when I met her. We both have made it a part of our life that we go visit Ms. Carol's grave and put fresh flowers out for her every week. We're both aware that no one blames us for her death, but we feel bad that it happened.

"Hey, handsome. When do you plan on telling the family?" Eva asked as she sat beside me on the bed.

"We can tell them tonight, but I would like to wait until after Cassie and Nas' wedding. Today is their day, and I would like to celebrate them."

Nasir and Cassie were finally getting married, and today was their wedding day. Cassie was undecided if she wanted a nice wedding or if she just wanted to go to the courthouse. The family planned a family vacation to St. Lucia, so they decided that they would do the ceremony here. I'm so happy for my sons. They both found beautiful wives that completed them. Their mother would be so proud of them, and she would've loved her daughter-in-laws.

"Ok, we have to get downstairs, the minister is here, and the ceremony is supposed to start in ten minutes," Eva said, and I stood pulling her into my arms.

"I love you, beautiful." I kissed her lips.

"I love you too, baby." She smiled, and we went downstairs to join the family. Priest rented this mansion for all of the family to stay together.

"Ma, you look beautiful," I said to my mother. She had finally welcomed Eva as a part of the family and loves going shopping with her. She finally let Mr. Joe move in with her, and he was actually here with us today. The only person that still gives them the side-eye is Nasir. But I'm just happy that she's happy. Priest and Zoey hired a nanny for their children, and they all love her. They never hired another chef, and I don't think they will.

"Hey, Pop. You look handsome," Zoey exclaimed as she walked downstairs.

"And you look beautiful as always, daughter. I can't wait to meet my granddaughter." I kissed her cheek.

"I can't wait to have her, so you can meet her," she

laughed. Zoey and Priest are expecting another child. She's five months pregnant, and this time around, she wanted to know what she was having.

"Pop-Pop, come onnn! We're getting married!" Sasha shouted, and we all laughed.

"She's been saying that all day." Priest shook his head, as he walked into the room with Priest Jr.

"Where is Nas?" I asked.

"He's on the patio with Cannon. I think they're getting ready to go down to the beach." Priest and I walked outside to join them, and they were already at the bar getting the party started.

"Bro, thank you for all of this. I was blessed when I got yo' ass as a brother. I had my son for free, I ate for free, and I'm getting married for free. You can't beat that shit," Nas told him, and all Priest could do was shake his head at his brother.

"Heyyyyy, y'all!" We all turned around and Tiff was standing there.

"Yoooo, you said you didn't know if you could make it. It's good to see you, cuz!" Nas pulled her in for a hug. We were all happy to see her. Tiff moved to California about a year ago. Cannon excused himself and walked away without speaking to her.

"Hey, cuz. We've missed you." Priest hugged her, and so did I.

"Britt, and I got in late last night." She smiled looking nervous as hell.

"Tiff, you know you're gonna have to make that shit right.

You fucked up. I'm not gone tell you how you should run your life, but on that situation, yo' ass was wrong, and I'm gone always tell you when you wrong," Nas told her, and she just looked into the direction of Cannon talking to his date that he came here with. Nasir stepped out of the game, and Cannon was doing a good job running the operation for us.

"It's time for the wedding to start, y'all need to go take your places. Take the boys down, they're going to sit with Big Mama," Zoey said as she came out and handed the boys off to us.

About twenty minutes later, we were all in our seats, and the wedding started. Priest stood next to his brother and smiled as his wife came walking down the aisle. *For you by Kenny Latimore* started playing and Cas came walking down with her mother. It was a small ceremony, but it was a very beautiful wedding. The sun was shining bright and, in my heart, I knew Bianca was here with her son today. I have never seen Nasir so happy. All he could do is smile, watching his bride come down.

"Hurry up, Bear! I'm ready to fu..." Priest nudged his brother, and we all laughed because we knew he was getting ready to say some off the wall shit. About thirty minutes later, the ceremony was coming to an end.

"I now pronounce you husband and wife. You may kiss your bride," the minister said to Nasir.

"Come here, Bear, and let me suck your face!" Nasir told and we all laughed.

"Ladies and gentlemen, I would like to introduce to you

Mr. & Mrs. Nasir Chamber!" The minister announced, and we all clapped. Everyone stood and rushed to congratulate them.

"Congrats to both of you. Cassie, welcome to the family." I smiled giving them both a hug. The rest of the family did the same, and a few minutes later, we all headed back to the house to celebrate. Later that night, we were all sitting out drinking and having a good time. I pulled Eva into my arms; this woman filled the hole that I had in my heart after I lost Bianca. Being with her gave me peace, and I knew that she was truly the woman for me.

"Everyone, I would like to have your attention for a moment. The loss of Bianca took a part of me and I had given up on life, thinking God had given up on me. It wasn't until I sat down and talked to my mother about how I was feeling. And she said to me that *'Sometimes God will shift a change in your life that you may never understand. Bianca was sick and God needed his child with him. Life doesn't always go the way we plan it, but you have to stand up, readjust yourself, and move forward.* She said *when it's time he will send you his creation, a woman he designed just for you.* Thank you for that advice mom. Priest and Nas we had a conversation a while ago about me moving on with, Eva and you both gave me your blessings. I love you boys more than I love myself, and I will always love your mother. You will never know what God did for me when he sent Eva into my life. Last month, when Eva and I went to St. Croix, we got married in a private cere-mony with just her and I. It just happened, it wasn't planned, but it was perfect and that's the way we both wanted it," I said to them and surprisingly no one was upset not even my mother.

"I should beat your ass, boy, but I'm happy you found love. Welcome to the family, daughter in-law," my mother stated, and my heart was at ease.

Everyone ran up to congratulate us, and I felt a sense of relief now that I've told my family. Eva and I were happy, and I loved this woman with everything in me. God has given me a second chance at love, and I'm eternally grateful.

The End

Get connected with Author K. Renee

To get VIP access of new releases, and sneak peeks please join my mailing list.

Text KRENEE to 22828

Website www.authorkrenee.com

Facebook: https://www.facebook.com/karen.renee.9421450

Instagram: http://www.instagram.com/Authorkrenee

Author K.Renee's Reading Group on FB: https://www.facebook.com/groups/1640789219356047/?ref=share

9 798662 783768